The Artisanal Grifter

In This Series

The Artisanal Grifter

The Artisanal Grifter

George Bixley

DAGMAR MIURA

LOS ANGELES

Published by Dagmar Miura
Los Angeles
www.dagmarmiura.com

The Artisanal Grifter

First published 2020

ISBN: 978-1-951130-41-1

ONE

¶¶¶¶¶¶¶¶¶¶¶

DORIS HAD ASKED SLATER to dinner, which wasn't too unusual, but on the phone she'd said she might have some work for him, and that was completely out of character. "I didn't raise you to be a pugilist," she'd told him, more than once, and he spared her the more lurid details of his career digging into insurance fraud and the lowlifes who perpetrated it. So tonight, sitting in a bustling Honduran place on Seventh Street downtown, eating a tamale with plantains on the side, he had to keep his curiosity in check.

Petite and with her dark hair showing some gray, Doris was animated as she told him a story about some nutty cousin from the East, waving her fork for emphasis. Even though they were inside, she was wearing jeans and a dark turtleneck for the chill of the winter evening. Finally Slater had a chance to ask.

"You said something about work."

"Right." She sat up and pushed her plate away, furrowing her brow, her expression serious now. "I have an old friend who needs help from someone with your kind of job experience."

Slater knew what she meant, the implication, even though she'd never say it. His beat was the dark side of the metropolis, and he knew how to maneuver in its gritty depths.

"What's his ask?"

"I'll let him tell you about it." She glanced at her phone on the table. "I actually invited him to eat with us. He said he'd join us after."

"Who is this guy?"

"Bud Morales. These days Councilmember Morales. He's a public figure."

"On the city council?" Slater frowned. "Why are you socializing with that kind of lowlife?"

"He's my friend. Early in my career we taught together. Bud didn't stick with it. He decided he was going to become a cop, and then he went to law school for a while, and now he's a politician. I actually live in his district."

Slater nodded. It was no surprise that Doris's neighborhood, on the heavily Latin east side of Los Angeles, would elect a Latin guy to represent them.

"What kind of person is he?"

"Bud's decent. Warm, and loyal to his friends. He's probably the most powerful person on city council right now—he's chair of the planning and land use committee. They call the shots for everything that gets built, from skyscrapers to backyard toolsheds."

"More powerful than the mayor?" Slater said.

"That putz just goes along with everything the committee comes up with. In return, they scratch his back when he asks."

Looking beyond his shoulder, Doris smiled and flashed her hand.

"Ibáñez," a deep voice boomed, and Slater turned to look.

Morales was dark, and burly, and wore a flashy brown suit. Slater was underdressed in comparison, in jeans and his black fake-leather jacket. But this guy probably wore a suit every single day. Doris rose long enough to exchange an air kiss with him, and as she sat down again, Morales turned to Slater.

"So this is your son. How did that happen?"

Slater scowled at him. He knew what he meant—Doris looked Anglo, but Slater had his father's dark Latin features, his black hair. If she wasn't sitting in front of him right now, he'd punch this idiot in the face.

"You knew Slater's father," Doris said. "You know he was Latino."

"That's not what I meant. How is it that you have a grown man for a son?" Morales gestured expansively. "It seems like a couple of weeks ago you and I were fresh out of college."

"Time is speeding up. I feel it too." She sat up in her chair. "Listen, if you two are going to talk, I don't need to be here."

"Always a pleasure, Doris." Morales stooped for a moment to embrace her. "Slater, I'll meet you in the bar," he said, and walked off.

Doris opened her handbag and gestured to the waitress.

"People totally recognize him," Slater said, watching Morales make his way across the restaurant, and pause to glad-hand the maître d', then nod in greeting to someone else across the room.

"This is Bud's town. We're just living in it."

The waitress handed her the check, and Doris paid her, then stood up. Slater rose too, and put a hand on her shoulder as he leaned in to kiss her good-bye.

"Love you," he said, and then headed toward the bar.

This end of the place wasn't busy, and Morales was the only person occupying a barstool.

"Slater," he boomed, in his big blustery voice. As if they hadn't seen each other in ages.

As Slater took an adjacent stool, Morales beckoned to the bartender, a slight twenty-something guy with lush dark hair, and ordered draft beer for both of them. At least he thought it was draft beer, as Morales ordered in Spanish, and Slater only understood snatches of the language.

After the bartender stepped away, Morales swiveled toward him.

"So Doris says you can handle rough characters."

"That might be overselling it. I'd say I'm familiar with lowlifes, and I can handle myself around them. I'm an insurance investigator."

"Does that mean you go take pictures of car accidents?"

"Not usually. The desk jockeys call me in when they have fieldwork that they can't handle themselves. I see lots and lots of fraud." Slater eyed him sidelong. "What is it that you need help with?"

The bartender set down two smalls of a pale lager, and Morales thanked him in loud effusive Spanish. Slater reached for one of the glasses, not bothering to dig out his cash. This guy had called the meeting and ordered the beer without consulting him, so he could damn well pay for it.

"Twelve fifty," the bartender said.

Morales dug in his pants pocket and produced a twenty, and set it on the bar, then clinked his glass on Slater's.

"First off, I'm a married man," Morales said.

"I can see that. You're wearing the handcuffs."

Morales sipped his beer. "Excuse me?"

"Your wedding ring."

He chuckled. "Right. I've got another election to win before I'm termed out on city council."

"What does that have to do with your marital status?"

Morales looked away and took a drink before he spoke. "It's kind of embarrassing."

"Don't get embarrassed," Slater demanded. "Just talk."

His eyebrows shot up. "OK. I was indiscreet with another woman. I'm concerned that if it becomes public, it might damage my reelection chances."

"This other woman wants money, or a job, or a political appointment?"

"Not her—a third party. It's definitely about money. There was specific mention of compromising photos, and a roll of film."

"They photographed you with her?" Slater said. "You were having sex?"

"I haven't seen all the images, but the seller sent a sample. They definitely nailed me. It's unmistakable what's going on."

"It strikes me as unusual that he'd use film. The blackmailer said that specifically? Film and not digital images?"

The seller is a woman. She sent me a digital image as bait. She's a photographer, right, so film is probably part of her business. Her name is Dawn Snowden."

"How much does Dawn Snowden want you to pay her for the film?"

"She hasn't given me a number yet," Morales said, "but I have a meeting with her at her studio tomorrow morning."

"And you want me to go with you."

"I want you to take the meeting for me. Find out what she wants."

"Do you intend to pay her?"

Morales sighed. "I don't think I have any other option."

"There are always options." Slater waved an arm. "You could send a message—burn down her freaking studio, or tow her car away and drop it over a cliff. Although personally I can't help you with that."

"I'm not that guy. I can't just throw gasoline on the fire."

"But you have to admit, it's entertaining to watch when someone does." Slater wrapped a hand around his glass. "So what's your budget?"

"Let's find out what she wants first. We'll negotiate from there. But I will say that I'm not a wealthy man."

"All right. I can go talk to her."

Morales nodded. "That would be great." Hoisting his beer again, he clinked it against Slater's. His face softened, like he was shifting out of blustery politician mode. It made his eyes look heavy.

Slater pulled his phone out of his jeans. "Where's the chiseler's studio?"

"Right on the edge of Skid Row. Los Angeles Street."

"How does she spell her name?" Slater thumb-typed a note to himself as Morales recited it. "And what about you? Do you have a direct line? No way am I dealing with your staff."

"My cell," Morales said, and rattled off the number.

Slater dug in his hip pocket to find a dog-eared business card, and handed it to him. "That's me."

"City hall is walking distance from this woman's photo studio," he said, tucking the card into his jacket. "I'll be in my office there tomorrow. You can drop by after you talk to her."

Slater slammed the last of his beer and then slid off the stool.

"I'll be in touch."

Morales swiveled to meet his gaze, an odd look in his eye. Veiled suspicion, maybe, or uncertainty. He extended a hand, and Slater shook it, working to match his iron grip.

"Thanks for your help."

"Save it," Slater said. "I haven't done anything yet."

Walking out to the street, he found his car, a classic 1970s Thunderbird, gleaming black and beautiful under the streetlights. Climbing in, he pulled into the traffic and headed west, across the chasm of the Harbor Freeway and into his neighborhood, squalid and impoverished Westlake.

As he pulled into the alley behind his building, his headlights caught a guy standing next to his garage, looking down, his hands at his crotch. The idiot was pissing on his door. Slater shifted into park and climbed out.

"Hey," he shouted, striding toward him.

The guy zipped his fly and turned around. He had shaggy hair and his clothes were rumpled, neither of which were unequivocal indicators of homelessness, but the shoes clinched it—he was wearing sneakers with no laces.

"What's your problem?" the guy demanded.

His eyes were bright, like he was wired, or high. Slater stepped up to him and slapped him hard on the face, then again on the other side, a rapid kovac. The guy flinched and tried to throw a punch, but his movements were predictable, and Slater easily blocked the blow, deflecting it with his forearm. With his other fist, Slater landed a solid gut punch, and the guy doubled over, then stumbled away from him, into the middle of the alley and then toward the side street.

"Don't piss here," Slater shouted after him. "Go do that in the park."

He watched the guy until he loped around the building at the end of the alley and out of view, then surveyed the garage door, illuminated by the headlights of the Thunderbird. A wet stain arced across the surface, and at the bottom was an ugly puddle. If he rolled the door up, it might run inside. He climbed into the Thunderbird again and drove to the side street, then up the block to a liquor store, where he pulled into the little lot and parked next to a prowl car.

Inside he walked to where the soft drinks were and found a gallon jug of water, then carried it to the till. In front of him was a uniformed cop, digging in his pocket. He produced a fin and set it on the counter next to a canned energy drink. The guy was tall, and well built, at least from this angle, beefy and with broad shoulders, and Slater studied the pleasing contours of his trousers.

He was only vaguely aware of the other cop, waiting for her partner a few feet away, near the entrance, but he looked up when she spoke.

"Can I help you with something?" She was looking right at him.

"I doubt it," Slater said.

The guy turned toward them as he pocketed his change, drink can in hand. He eyed Slater as he stepped past him and put the water jug on the counter next to the till.

"What's going on?"

"He was eyeing your sidearm," the woman said.

"Bullshit," Slater said. "I was looking at his ass."

The guy put his hands on his belt. "That's totally inappropriate."

"What, you wear your uniform that tight so people won't look?" Slater pulled his wad of cash out of his front pocket and set a C-note on the counter, then gestured toward the guy's feet. "Plus those fuck-me boots. Come on."

"Don't be disrespecting the police," the woman said.

Slater frowned. "There's nothing I respect more than a hot guy, police or otherwise."

The cop briefly lifted his foot in front of him and looked at it. "These are regulation."

"Let's just go," the woman said, then jutted her chin at Slater. "Watch your mouth."

"You don't need to be shy about being hot," Slater called after them, then muttered, "Idiot."

"Anything else?" the clerk said, struggling to suppress a smile.

"Give me two bottles of the black label." Slater gestured to the shelf behind him, to the brand of bourbon he always bought. It wasn't the best quality stuff, but he drank enough of it that he couldn't afford to go upscale.

Plastic bag in hand, he went out to his car and drove back to his alley. There was no sign of the doper. Parked at an angle, with his headlights illuminating the garage door, he climbed out and poured water from the jug onto the door. Worse things probably happened here when he wasn't around, but it was satisfying to wash most of it toward the shallow swale in the middle of the alley.

Climbing into the Thunderbird, he waited for the heavy door to roll up. This big private garage was the main reason he kept this crummy apartment—it was a rarity in the crowded central neighborhood.

Before he nosed the car inside, he glanced up and down the alley. No way did he want that doper or any of the other homeless locals to sneak in behind him; he'd have another scuffle on his hands.

He splashed the last of the water in the jug on the threshold, then waited for the door to roll down before he went through the back and trotted up the two flights to his dingy one-bedroom. The main room had a kitchen counter at one end, and a couple of pieces of thrift-store furniture at the other, with a grimy window that looked out on the street.

Setting the bourbon bottles beside the kitchen sink, he stooped to pull off his boots, then killed the lights and stretched out in his recliner. The booze was waiting patiently for him, amber and lovely and loyal. He could feel it. But guys came before booze—otherwise things got muddled.

Slater dug out his phone and opened the hookup app, and swiped through the images of torsos and other body parts. He paused at the head shot of a swarthy guy, built thick and with slick dark hair, and that same broad nose as Morales. The resemblance wasn't coincidental—this guy probably came from one of the same extended families on the ranchos in Durango and Sinaloa. Slater sent him a concise message:

I want to fuck you. My place only. No drugs.

His reply came a moment later:

The app says you're 0.3 miles away. Send me your address and I'll walk over.

Slater thumb-typed it, then got up and went into his bedroom, shuffling the covers onto his futon and kicking his dirty laundry into the bottom of the closet. Before he had time to put on a clean shirt, there was a tentative knock at the front door.

When he pulled it open, the guy beamed at him and said something in Spanish.

"*No comprendo,*" Slater said, making the vowels sound as drawn-out and Anglo as he could.

"I said you look like your photo."

"You look younger than yours."

"Is that a good thing?"

"Come in." Slater closed the door behind him.

Maybe he did look like his photo, but he was younger than Morales. Standing close to him, he grasped the guy's biceps and felt his musculature.

"So what do you like to do?"

"I don't really have a specific sex thing."

"Yeah, you do," Slater said, putting his hands on his hips. "Everyone does. You don't have to dance around it. I'm the guy you can explain it to."

"Well, what about you? You said you wanted to fuck me."

"It's just an expression. But we can do that."

Leaning in, Slater met his warm mouth, exploring it. The guy moved closer and ran his hands over his back. Slater grabbed the sides of his belt and pulled him closer, so he could feel his wood. Pulling back, the guy took a breath, that look of anticipation in his eye, and peeled off his shirt. Slater ran his hands over his chest and then led him to the bedroom. He pulled off his own shirt and unbuckled his belt.

"Let me," the guy said, and sat on the edge of the bed, sliding his own pants off, revealing a raging woody, and then pulled the fly of Slater's jeans open. He grasped Slater's cock, and took it into his mouth, and spent a minute working it. Slater spread his feet apart and watched.

"You have to stop," Slater said finally, breathing hard. "I'm close."

"Why stop?" he said, and went back to it.

A moment later Slater came, and grabbed his head between his hands to steady him, shuddering with the intensity. The guy looked up at him, grinning, and grabbed his forearm to pull him onto the bed. Rolling on top of him, he pressed his wood into Slater's belly.

"Can I fuck you?" he said.

"Sure." Slater reached for the bedside table and grabbed a condom, and rolled it on for him, then squeezed his cock, eliciting a gasp.

Shifting down the bed, he grabbed the lube and deftly worked his way into Slater, then pushed his knee higher, and penetrated him. The guy was confident for someone his age, Slater thought, watching him maneuver. Soon he was pounding him, and then he came, straining into him, breathing hard. Pulling away, he flipped onto his back.

Slater let him draw his forearm under his neck, then folded his other arm over his eyes. He'd just started to drift off when the guy got up. The sound of water running came from the bathroom, and when he returned, he started to pull on his clothes.

"You can hang out, if you want," Slater said, watching him in the dim light. "I'll be asleep."

"My mom gets worried if I stay out too late."

"Of course. We wouldn't want that."

Slater rose and followed him to the front door, and after an awkward kiss, locked the bolt as he left.

He liked this part of the day, with the sex behind him, feeling satisfied for a while. Since he was in for the night, his booze rules said he could start drinking. Another fifth of bourbon sat in the kitchen cupboard, almost empty, and he swapped it for the ones he'd brought in this evening, then poured his ration into a tumbler, eyeballing the one-inch level.

It was annoying to have to keep track, but this was one of the revised booze rules. Right now it was the only way he could keep Doris and his idiot ex-boyfriend, Conrad, from bundling him off to some organic-hemp rehab facility. He could imagine the kind of place they'd put him in—he'd have to dry out and sit around talking about his feelings with a bunch of damn addicts, under the stern watch of some ageing caftan-clad hippie.

He slammed his ration and relished the burn in his throat, the heady fumes in his nose. It didn't seem fair that this was all there was. He poured another inch or so, then killed the lights and sat in his recliner. The warmth was growing in his belly, starting to suffuse his body. He had to smile. This was when his mind finally started to slow down, disengage, unspool. This was the best part of the day.

TWO

DAYLIGHT STREAMED IN THE narrow window above Slater's bed when he woke. He wasn't sure how he'd got here, or when, but he was alone. The guy had left, he remembered. His head didn't hurt, and that meant this was a good morning.

There was never anything to eat in the icebox, but he pulled open the door to look inside anyway, just in case he'd missed something. He screwed the top off the pickle jar and fished out a few spears, then munched on them as he went to get dressed. It was supposed to be in the high sixties today, warm for January, so he pulled on a long-sleeved shirt, and buttoned it, and tucked it in, but didn't bother with a jacket. Minutes later, he trotted down the two flights to his garage, and backed the Thunderbird into the alley, and drove to Skid Row.

Los Angeles Street was the green line between

the grinding homeless poverty of Skid Row and the renovated Historic Core, where the tony lofts and condos and restaurants were only for the wealthy. Up the block from the address Morales had given him, he found an open meter space and pulled in.

Most of the businesses on this stretch were clothing retailers. When he walked up on the black-mailer's photo studio, he didn't have to check the number—painted on the glass door in blocky gold lettering was DAWN SNOWDEN PHOTOGRAPHY. The storefront had no windows, and a heavy steel shutter was rolled up just above the entrance, poised to protect the place from the chaotic neighborhood after business hours.

Next to the entrance the facade bore a mural, a swirling knot of abstract red ribbons, signed at the bottom with what looked like a street artist's tag. It was a smart move to prevent unwanted graffiti—only a total dick would tag over an existing artwork, and if the artist was one of the thousands of people sleeping rough in this neighborhood, he'd likely defend the mural himself.

As Slater pulled open the door, he saw that the walls inside bore a series of blown-up black-and-white photos of a stick-thin model in a rumpled sack-like dress. The poses were intentionally awkward, some childish, some flirtatious, most with the dress askew. It was an uncomfortable combination, the juvenile and the sexy, but that was probably the point. Who would buy this stuff?

He scanned the room. There were no cameras anywhere. It was unusual for a retailer not to have security, especially in this neighborhood, but then there didn't look to be much to steal in here—and it was smart not to have surveillance if you were trying to grift a politician.

Behind the counter was a guy with unkempt black hair pulled into a bundle behind his head. In his twenties, maybe, he didn't look up when Slater walked in.

Stepping farther inside, Slater casually glanced into the two doorways that led to other rooms. One was a photo lab, with oversize trays for the chemical baths to make prints, and on a table a towering photo enlarger. That's likely what had created the big prints on the walls.

The other door was half closed, but he could see the corner of a desk and a file cabinet. It didn't look cluttered, but it wasn't too controlled either, with a pile of paper on the desk, the top drawer of the cabinet left open.

"*No baños,*" the clerk said, finally acknowledging him.

"What?"

"We don't have a public restroom."

"Fuck you, you little punk. I'm not homeless."

The guy looked him up and down. "Are you sure about that?"

Slater stepped close to the counter. The guy flinched and stepped back, but not before Slater managed to strike him with a quick right to the jaw. His head snapped sideways. Turning back, he glared at him, surprise and anger in his eyes.

"You punched me. That's assault."

"That's actually what's called an attention-grabber. It won't even leave a bruise, you big baby."

"I'm calling the cops."

"Go for it," Slater said. "I'll tell them you hit me first. And I'm really good with cops."

The clerk frowned, unsure now.

"You could always show them your security video." Slater gestured around at the ceiling. "Except you forgot to put in the cameras."

A woman stepped out of the back office, a scowl on her face. She was on the far side of forty, with pale blue eyes and dried-out peroxide-blond hair that fell to her shoulders. Her eyes flicked over Slater's form.

"What's all the shouting?"

"This homeless freak hit me," the clerk said. "I'm calling the cops."

"That's a lie," Slater said flatly.

"Nobody's bringing the cops in here," she said, raising her voice. "Just chill out."

"I have an appointment with Dawn Snowden," Slater said. "I assume that's you."

"You're not who I was expecting."

"I'm representing him."

"Interesting."

As she stepped closer to the counter, her eyes went soft, and she flipped her hair with her fingers, and dropped her chin. That wasn't something he saw very often anymore—old-school coquette moves. Dawn leaned on the counter, her palms wide apart, and craned her neck so that he could see into her blouse.

"You know, you don't really have the cleavage to pull that off," Slater said.

The clerk audibly stifled a laugh, and Dawn stood erect, her brow furrowing.

"It's not a big deal to get them augmented," Slater said. "You're blond and Anglo and live in LA. Why wouldn't you get implants?"

"You're kind of an asshole," she said evenly, then looked at the clerk. "Why don't you go get your lunch?"

"I just got here," he said.

"Go get a coffee, then. I need a few minutes."

The guy huffed and stepped around the counter, then walked out the front door to the street.

"Your staff doesn't know you're a blackmailer?"

"I'm a businesswoman. You don't look like a typical city hall toady."

Slater pulled a business card out of his hip pocket and set it on the counter in front of her. Dawn picked it up and read it.

"Ibáñez? Is that Mexican?" She looked up at him. "This says you're in insurance. Why are you working for Morales?"

"I'm just a go-between."

"Has he authorized you to pay me?"

Slater put his hands on his hips. "How much do you want from him for the photos?"

"The buyer can make me an offer."

"That's not how this works."

"I am curious as to how much the pictures are worth to the councilmember." A smile played on her lips, and she dropped her chin again. "He's seen how explosive they are."

"You sent him a photo, but you also said they were on a roll of film."

"Film is the standard medium. I emailed him a digital sample to get his attention."

Slater gestured impatiently. "How about a thousand bucks?"

Dawn hooted, throwing her head back, then braced her palms on the counter. "Oh, *cholo*, you're operating on a different level of reality."

"Normally I'd be offended at that label," Slater said, keeping his tone calm. "But coming from an entitled white person, I know you don't really know what that word means."

"I'm not entitled."

"It's built in, toots, being as white as you are."

She raised her eyebrows. "You don't know anything about me."

"You're so white you disappear against the wall behind you. All I see are two wrinkly pinholes that I assume must be your eyes."

"Get out of my store," she snapped.

Slater didn't budge. "You need to tell me what you want. Otherwise this transaction is going nowhere."

"Tell the councilmember we'll start with fifty grand for the roll of film."

"You just said you have digital copies. Are you going to destroy those as part of the deal?"

"Fifty is the first payment on me keeping quiet."

"The installment plan." Slater nodded. "Got it."

He walked out to the street and headed to his

car. It would be easy to walk the few short blocks to city hall, like Morales suggested, but no way was he going to leave his wheels on the fringe of Skid Row, even in broad daylight. Waiting for a break in the traffic, he pulled a U-turn and drove toward the Civic Center. There was no street parking anywhere around here, so he pulled into the lot under the courthouse.

Walking up on city hall, he realized he'd never really looked at the place, even though he drove by here sometimes. The grounds around the iconic structure were planted with mature *rubiginosa* ficus trees and towering Mexican *washingtonias*. Both were lousy landscaping choices, as they were introduced species. But in another sense, maybe they did fit—at its core, this was a colonized place. The Spanish had colonized the first people, then the Anglos colonized them both. Maybe that's what the planners were trying to convey a century ago when they built this grand tower.

Some of the ficus trees already had black blotches on the bark, evidence of the fungus that was slowly killing them all, already spread throughout the metropolis. Maybe that was appropriate too—the blight symbolic of the rot inside this building.

Once he'd hustled up the wide white steps and into the luxy columned foyer, he spoke to the guard at the security counter, a chunky guy with oily hair, clad in a dark uniform.

"Where's Bud Morales's office?"

The guy frowned. "You can't just walk in there."

"I'm expected."

"I have to check on that. Do you have a photo ID?"

Slater huffed in frustration and pulled out his driver's license.

The guard eyed it and spent a moment clacking at his computer keyboard. "You're not on his visitor list."

"That's not my freaking problem," Slater said, raising his voice. "I have a meeting with him. Where's his office?"

Keeping his eye on him, the guard picked up his phone and punched at the number pad. Slater glared at him, drumming his fingers on the counter-top. After a brief conversation, the guard hung up.

"Fourth floor," he said, handing his license back, and recited the suite number.

"Great job keeping the politicians safe from the electorate," Slater said, and walked toward the elevators.

Once he was upstairs, walking the wide hall, he saw Morales step out of a doorway, wearing the same slick brown suit he'd had on last night. Several doors down from the number the guard had given him, this door was styled in baroque dark wood, but it was unmarked. When he spotted Slater, Morales waved him in.

This was his private office, with a lush uphol-stered lounge suite at the far end, and closer to this door a wide desk and a bookcase of uniform red-bound volumes—law books that no one ever looked at. In a corner behind the desk was a city flag on a stand. With its green and gold panels and jagged lines, to Slater it had always felt more like a minor African nation's flag than something representative of this crazy city. He glanced around as he stepped inside and waited for Morales to close the door. The dark wood all around and the cushy chairs made it look a lot like a lawyer's office.

Morales eased into the chair behind his desk and gestured to one in front of it. As he sat, Slater could see it now—the flag was positioned just behind Morales's shoulder, a setup for video messages or photo ops of the councilmember at his desk, hard at work.

"Dawn's plan is to bleed you over time," Slater said. "For the first installment, she wants fifty grand."

Morales sat up. "Are you kidding me? I can't afford that kind of money. Especially if she's going to ask for more. I'm not a wealthy man."

"She seems to think otherwise."

"My income here is less than three hundred."

"Thousand?" Slater demanded. "A year?"

"Right."

"I guess that makes sense. You people get to set your own salaries."

Morales waved dismissively. "It's not fair, Slater. One slip, one little dalliance, and it's going to ruin me. The end of my career."

You should have considered that when you were climbing into bed with another woman, Slater thought. But he didn't say that.

"If you want, I can look into Dawn. I might get something to throw back at her, and slow her down."

"That would be helpful." Morales's eyes narrowed. "But you can't burn down her studio."

"That's not my style. I'm an investigator—I'll do some digging. But the part where I'm doing Doris a favor is over. You're going to have to pay me."

"Of course." Morales gestured amiably. "How much do you get paid?"

"Give me three grand, and I'll spend the next few days on Dawn."

He sat up and opened the bottom drawer of his desk.

"I also want to see the photo she sent," Slater said.

"No, man—it's embarrassing." Morales rummaged in the drawer, then pulled out a stack of cash. The bills were folded in half and bound with a blue elastic band. Rising for a moment, he reached across the desk and set the bundle on the edge next to Slater.

"That should be five grand," Morales said. "See what you can dig up for that."

"I thought you weren't a wealthy man."

"My wife and I own a few commercial properties. Some of the tenants pay the rent in cash."

"Are you sure about that?" Slater said. "That's how drug dealers store their money."

Morales laughed, his tone deep. "It's nothing like that."

"Maybe your tenants are drug dealers."

"They're legitimate small business owners who happen to deal in cash."

Slater rose and stuffed the green wad into his

hip pocket.

"I knew you were the right guy for the job," Morales said, and stood up. "I could tell when we met."

"Let's see what happens."

"Listen." He stepped closer, and held Slater's gaze. "Whatever you do, you have to keep my name out of the media."

"And you have to keep your dick in your pants."

Not waiting for a reply, Slater walked out the side door, and strode the hallway to the elevators, and rode down to the street.

THREE

T HE OFFICE THAT SLATER shared with Max, his business partner, was just a few minutes' drive, in the Fashion District, in an old office building that had mostly been converted into sewing factories. They collaborated on jobs sometimes, the labor-intensive stakeouts and strong-arm work, but mostly they just shared resources. Max was a licensed PI, and that gave Slater access to some useful stuff.

Pulling into the surface lot across the street, he was glad to see Max's matte-gray Challenger parked a few spaces down. Slater hustled across in a break in the traffic and strode into the lobby. Early in the day there were usually gig laborers hanging around, waiting for work in the building's clothing factories, sewing or cutting or carting garments, and he stepped past a few of them and rode up to the ninth floor. As he walked around behind the elevator shaft, he admired their names on the door:

SLATER IBÁÑEZ
MAXIMILLIAN CONROY
INVESTIGATIONS

Inside was a small office for each of them, and in between a front office with a coat rack and a reception desk that no one ever used. The only decoration was parked on the desktop—a small statue of Rey Pascual, a skeleton wearing a crown and holding a scythe. It had been a gift from the woman who sold him *pupusas,* meant to bring something beneficial, luck or success or good health.

Max was in his office, sitting behind his desk. His mousy brown hair was thinning, and he had a little weight on his frame, with his sidearm bulging under his suit jacket. The whole package made his profession unmistakable: Max was the heavy. Today he was wearing his dark red suit and a lustrous red necktie. That meant he was meeting with someone and needed to project authority—interviewing a reluctant witness or presenting a client with his bill.

"Have you got a minute?" Slater said, standing in his doorway.

Max waved to the guest chair. "Sit down."

This was what he liked about Max—the guy was never impatient, always had time for Slater, always had time to talk. Sometimes he wanted to punch him in the face, but Slater felt that way about most people. With Max he had a rapport, the trust they'd built from working together.

"Can you look up someone for me in one of your databases?"

Max sat up and pulled his keyboard closer with a meaty hand. "Shoot."

"Her name is Dawn Snowden."

His stubby fingers banged at the keyboard. "Are you working a case?"

"This woman is trying to chisel a friend of Doris's. I'm not sure where I'm at with him, though—he's already lied to me about parts of it."

"You know I'm a Doris fan," Max said, absorbed in the screen. "How is she?"

"Same as always."

His eyes narrowed, peering at the computer. "I can only find one local person with that name spelled that way."

"It might be my target. She has a photo business on Los Angeles Street."

"Then we've got her. Dawn Snowden is actually an alias. Her legal name is Dawn Strezlecki." He clicked the mouse and moved it around. "Ms. Strezlecki spent a year in a rest home."

"Seriously? What was she sent up for?"

"A fraud rap. I can't see the case specifics here, but the sentence was three years. She was at the women's state prison in the Central Valley. Paroled after one year … still on parole." He looked up. "Do you need contact details?"

"If her home address is there, email it to me. Also the spelling of her legal name."

Max nodded and spent a moment typing, then looked up. "So she's running a blackmail scam?"

"Correct," Slater said, and rose.

"That never ends well."

"Not if I can help it. Thanks, buddy."

Stepping across into his own office, Slater grabbed the pile of mail from the corner of his desk and leafed through it. Nothing looked too urgent, so he pulled out Morales's wad of cash and sat down to go through it.

The bills were a random assortment of used twenties and hundreds, exactly like what a drug dealer would have. Counting out two grand, he turned to the safe that was bolted to the floor behind his desk, and got it open, and put the remaining three in the envelope he and Max used for rent and petty cash. On the outside, Slater added a note to the bottom of the list of deposits and withdrawals:

Slater—deposit—3G

The accountant they'd hired to take care of their taxes hated the way they handled money, but it was inevitable—lots of their clients didn't want a paper trail to a pair of private investigators, so they paid in cash.

Pulling his keyboard into his lap, Slater heaved his boots up on the desk and did a web search for Dawn Snowden. Apart from hits for her photo studio, nothing came up about her. One listing explained that she did head shots, photo shoots, and printing. There was no mention anywhere of the fraud conviction.

He pulled up Max's email and copied her legal name, Dawn Strezlecki. Several people with that handle appeared in the search results, including one who worked for the state government of Pennsylvania, one who was an aspiring stand-up comic at a performing arts high school, and somebody from Fresno whose social-media profile photo showed that she had twenty years and thirty pounds on his target.

Clearly Dawn kept a low profile. Slater locked his computer with a keystroke and set the keyboard on his desk, then stretched and folded his arms over his head, eyeing the faded painting on the wall next to his office door. It was his one attempt at decorating this place. Three artichokes in a bowl. He didn't give a damn about artichokes, but he'd found it cheap at a thrift store. It had seemed appropriate at the time.

What he needed was to find out more about Dawn's business. What was she up to, and who else was she grifting? The angle he could use was evident—he already had an in with her. Rising from his chair, he called good-bye to Max as he walked out.

———◆———

AFTER HE TROTTED ACROSS the street between the oncoming vehicles, he climbed into the Thunderbird and navigated toward the freeway. It was still early in the afternoon, but Friday traffic was already making the roads sluggish, and it took a while to get to Glendale.

Exiting onto surface streets, Slater headed to the seedy part of town, where Svetlana and her brother, the duo who sold him all his illicit tech, had their workshop. Their gear was clunky and the interface sometimes involved a language gap, but it worked so well that he never had to go anywhere else.

He parked in front of their building, a long one-story with a sagging roofline, painted that pink-tan color used on so many commercial structures. The windows were heavily barred, and the front door probably hadn't been opened in years. Cameras covered both directions along the sidewalk out front. Svetlana or her staff had likely identified him the moment he'd pulled up. Slater walked to the end of the building and onto the side street, then into the alley behind. This was where the real entrance was, a heavy steel door with a camera aimed at him from above. He looked up into the lens and smiled.

The door lock buzzed, and he pulled it open and stepped into the anteroom. Here he faced another heavy locked door, and stood with his feet apart, his hands away from his sides. They'd installed some kind of body scanner in here, more sophisticated than a metal detector, and as he waited he wondered idly what kind of radiation dose he was getting right now—Svetlana wasn't bound by any health regulations, not subject to citation or admonishment by any inspector. He must have passed muster, as the inner door buzzed open, and he pushed his way inside.

The workshop had narrow high windows along two of the walls, but the long workbenches were lit mostly by dangling fluorescent fixtures. The place smelled like solder and hot plastic and machine oil.

Svetlana was parked on a stool at one of the workbenches. Behind her a computer screen showed a grayscale image of a human form, legs apart, arms at its sides. That was a scan of his own body, he realized.

Svetlana swiveled around to greet him. She was wearing a skirt plastered with a vibrant sunflower print and a bright orange top. It was cut low in front—clearly she wasn't shy about showing her ample cleavage. Svetlana always dressed like she was ready for a stroll through a flower market on the Riviera, not for close work in a dark little factory in the gray California winter. It was hard to pin down her age, but she was likely in her fifties.

"*Dobraye utro,*" Slater said.

Svetlana laughed. "Your pronunciation is good. Try again." She repeated the phrase, and waited for him to say it. "Nice," she said finally. "The only problem is that it's not morning. So you should say, "*Dobraye den.*"

Slater repeated that, his tongue tripping over the *r* sound.

She made him practice it a few more times, then nodded, satisfied. "You could fool even an FSB agent."

"Not for long."

"So—your subscriptions are all paid up. You're seeking something new?"

"I need an audio bug that I can plant in a retail shop. I won't have a chance to be alone there, so it has to be something I can leave behind."

She slid off her stool. "For this, I have many."

Slater followed her to the far wall, where a long shelving unit was cluttered with an array of parts—green circuit boards, bales of wire, molded plastic components.

"Are you still working alone?" he said. "I haven't seen Igor in ages."

She waved a hand. "He's away."

He'd heard that before, and with the language gap he was never sure if she meant he was traveling, or incarcerated, or something else.

"You mean overseas?"

Svetlana eyed him. "Do you know Siberia?"

"I know where it is. I've never been there."

"I want him to come back, but he says he's on a personal quest. I call it a psychological debility."

"That seems like a strange place to do it."

She shrugged. "He speaks the language, so in some ways it's easy. I think one more winter there and he'll be finished with it." From the shelf she took what looked like a short strip of duct tape, bending it and then handing it to him. "Inside the ribbon is a flexible flat battery. The microphone is concealed right here. You can stick it on any-thing—a storage box, or a car, or a piece of furni-ture. The battery works for ten days."

"I need to listen in on a retail shop," Slater said, handing it back. "The place is pretty tidy—I don't know where I'd put it."

"What about this?"

She handed him a coffee mug, with LA printed on it in thick black letters. The electronics and the battery were in the base, he decided, as it looked a lot thicker than on a standard mug.

"This could work," he said. "What else have you got?"

Next she handed him a paper coffee cup, its waxy rim crumpled and stiffly glued shut.

"All the electronics are inside," she said. "It looks like trash, so no one is going to pry it open."

"But it could easily get thrown away."

"True. Most of these audio devices you'll have to sacrifice. But they're much cheaper than video cameras."

"I assume none of them are traceable if someone figures out what they are."

Svetlana frowned. "You know me better than that. It's only going to be traceable if you leave your own fingerprints on it. That would fall into the category of not my problem." She reached for a little pocket calculator. "How about this? It can even do real arithmetic."

"It's heavy," Slater said, assessing its heft in his palm.

"For the battery. Most people won't be suspicious of that. It's also something you would throw in a drawer, not in the garbage. You can put it in a corner, or on a shelf, where it won't be noticed."

He eyed the little gray readout. The LCD zero flickered when he pressed the CLEAR button. "This is the one."

"I'll connect it to your accounts." She took it from him and walked back to her computer. "It will record and upload any sounds, so you don't have to listen in real time."

"How does that work?"

"You'll get an alert from my app when there's a new recording."

"It uses the cell network?"

"Correct. I've also connected the software to public transcription systems, so you can read the conversation instead of listening to it."

"That sounds extremely useful."

"It takes a few minutes to process, however," she said, turning away from the screen to meet his gaze. "I piggybacked on the free commercial services. That means the data has to look anonymous and random. I had to write a lot of code."

Next to her computer, she picked up a wand with a glowing red tip and swiped it across the bar code sticker on the back of the calculator, then peeled the sticker off and crumpled it into a ball. She spent a minute with her keyboard, staring at the computer screen's blue glow. From where he stood, Slater couldn't see what was on it, as the screen had some kind of directional filter.

"Done—it will appear in your accounts. Let me show you the power switch." She picked up the calculator again and pointed out a tiny sliding switch on the edge of the device. "The arithmetic chip works any time, but the microphone and the cellular radio to transmit data need more power. Don't activate it until you're ready to use it. It should transmit for at least a week."

"What do I owe you?" Slater said, and pulled out his wad of cash.

"For a regular customer, one dollar."

He peeled off a C-note and handed it over. It quickly disappeared into her cleavage.

"You're a genius," Slater said, and waggled the calculator before he tucked it in his pocket.

"Stop this kind of talk."

"I mean it. Your stuff is the best."

She shrugged. "If you're happy, I'm happy."

"Dosvidaniya."

Svetlana laughed and repeated the phrase back to him.

FOUR

TRAFFIC WAS CONGESTED ON the way down-town, but eventually Slater was close to Dawn's studio, and pulled into a meter space a block away. From the trunk of his car he took his canvas satchel and dropped the calculator into it, then slung it over his shoulder.

When he strode into the photo studio, the same belligerent clerk was behind the counter, talking to a woman standing across from him. A set of photo prints was arrayed on the countertop between them, and the guy was explaining something technical to her. This idiot was a total slouch—he didn't even look up when Slater came in.

Walking farther into the space, he stood where he could see into Dawn's office. The door was wide open, and she was behind her desk. He jutted his chin at her when she looked up. Her lip twisted into a sneer as she registered who he was.

"I have a counteroffer," Slater called to her, loud enough so the clerk and the customer would hear him.

Dawn quickly rose and hustled out to the counter, glancing sidelong at her employee.

"Come into my office," she said, scowling at him, and closed the door behind them when he stepped in.

"You don't want your photo customers to know you're a grifter?" Slater dropped into the seat in front of her desk and shifted his satchel into his lap.

"I don't share all my business with the help." She sat behind her desk and scooted the chair forward, flipping her dried-out blond hair back and then folding her arms on the desktop. "What do you want?"

"I spoke to my client. He's willing to offer you fifty grand if you give me all the copies of the photos, and let me watch you permanently delete your backups."

Dawn blinked several times and then scoffed. "Do you think I'm stupid?"

Slater leaned toward the desk and raised his eyebrows. "That's a loaded question." As he moved, he slid his hand into his satchel and palmed the little calculator. He found the recessed power switch and clicked it on with his fingernail.

"I'm not going to do that," Dawn said, and waved her arm. "Your boss has buckets of money."

"That's why we're at fifty grand." Shifting in his chair, he pulled the calculator out of the satchel, and concealed it in his hand.

"Why would I kill the cow if I can keep drinking the milk?"

"That analogy doesn't really resonate. I'm vegan."

Her brow furrowed. "You? Seriously?"

"It's not just for affluent Anglos," he snapped, sitting up. At the same time, he tossed the calculator under her desk, toward the side, where it would hopefully land under the drawers. It made no sound as it struck the carpet.

Her eyes fixed on him, Dawn didn't notice what he'd done. "Did anyone ever tell you that you have issues?"

"The popular classes have morals too, when they can afford them."

"Something about you doesn't quite fit with 'popular classes,'" she said, "although you seem to want to present yourself that way."

"Have you heard of the blackmailer's ultimate reward?"

"I'd say that would be lots and lots of money."

"A shallow grave out in the Mojave Desert, or up in the San Gabriel Mountains."

"Are you threatening me?"

"You're too much of a lowlife to feel threatened, Dawn. We both know that. The fact that you're sitting here means you managed to keep yourself from getting shanked during that stint at Chowchilla."

Her eyebrows shot up. "Are you stalking me?"

"Do you think I wasn't going to do my homework? Prison time is public record. I didn't need to look very hard to find out that you're garbage."

"Fuck you," she snapped.

"You're garbage, Dawn. You need to accept that." He rose and moved toward the door.

"Maybe I'll publish those pictures of your boss. I'll put them up on every social media platform I can find."

Slater looked back. "You can do that, if you want. But then your payoff is zero. You'd be killing the cow before you even got any milk." He stepped to the doorway, then turned back, as if he'd just remembered. "Does madam have a counteroffer?"

"Sixty grand by Monday."

"I'll relay the message, but your rates are going in the wrong direction."

Walking up the block to his car, Slater had to grin. The carpet in her office didn't look very clean, which meant it didn't get vacuumed very often. Even if a cleaner found the calculator, it would likely wind up tossed on a shelf or in a drawer, like Svetlana had said.

He drove the few blocks to the Fashion District and parked across the street from his office. The parking attendant waved from the little booth as he climbed out. Those people rarely bugged him— he bought a monthly pass, and they recognized his distinctive vehicle.

The lights were off when he got upstairs, and once he'd flicked them on, he stepped into Max's office to make sure no one was here. He eyed the statue on the front desk as he walked across to his own space.

"Just you and me, Rey."

Once he was sitting at his computer, he checked

on Svetlana's software. Sure enough there was a new device listed, the calculator bug, and a notification from it labeled "audio sound." That specific combination of words didn't make a lot of sense, but then most of her software was a jumble of broken English and Cyrillic. Even though Svetlana spoke fluent English, she likely subcontracted some of her software to programmers in the motherland.

He clicked on the notice, and it pulled up a link to a recording and a transcript of part of the conversation he'd just had with Dawn, from the point where he'd activated the bug. It was strange to see his own words transcribed: *You're garbage, Dawn. You need to accept that.*

As he stared at the screen, an alert popped up, a bubble that read "обнаружен," soon replaced by "processing …." The bug had picked up a new conversation, and it was happening right now. A moment later the first part of the transcript appeared: "A can under sand wire please on actual film."

That was nonsensical—something was getting garbled. He clicked on the audio file to listen. It was Dawn speaking, plus a man's voice, but not her idiot counter clerk. This guy's voice was deeper, and he had a speech impediment. That might explain why the transcription software had messed up.

"Hey, pretty lady," the guy said.

"Spare me your sexist bullshit," Dawn said. "Do you have the film?"

"I can't understand why you bother putting this stuff on actual film. It's so much work."

"It needs to be tangible. The suckers need something to hold in their sad little hands. It gives them catharsis to have physical evidence that they can destroy."

"If you ever actually give it to them."

"That's not your business," she said.

"How did it go with the politician?"

"He sent a thug, and he tried to lowball me. But he'll get there once the surprise wears off. I suspect he just needs a day or so to ruminate on what my product is really worth."

"What about the Samoan?" the guy said.

"I know she'll be around the cathedral today. I want to talk to her in person, but I've got other things to do."

"Want me to go over there and have a word? I could lay down the law. Tell her what's what."

"That's not your job," Dawn said, her tone sharp. "Don't forget who's the boss. You need to keep the websites running, and get me those rolls of film."

"Jesus, woman—cool your jets. They're almost ready. I'll bring them over tomorrow. And you know you owe me some money."

"You'll get paid when the politician pays. Just bring me the damn film."

"Sure, sure," he said, his voice fading, as if he'd stepped out of her office.

"You'd damn well better be here when the shop opens," Dawn shouted after him.

That was the end of the recording. Slater stared absently at the old painting of the artichokes, listening to the distant bass thrum of sewing machines in the factories down the hall. These two weren't amicable, but they knew each other well. That meant Dawn had help with the grift. If she wasn't able to pay the guy what she owed him, that meant money was tight—a situation that could make people desperate. Maybe he'd be able to leverage that.

They'd also revealed that there were other victims—Dawn was blackmailing someone who hung around the cathedral. That place had cheap parking, he knew, and it wasn't far.

Once he'd locked up the office, he made his way down to the street, and climbed into his car, and drove to the cathedral. It was perched on Bunker Hill, at the edge of downtown, looming above the freeway. The parking lot was almost empty when he pulled in.

Strolling out into the courtyard, he eyed the stand of king palms. Those weren't native, but then neither was Catholicism. Those stupid showy things came from the other side of the planet, Australia or Brazil or South Africa, maybe, as removed from California as the hub of the church's empire in Italy. Why couldn't people just look at what was already growing here and embrace it? At least the palms were healthy, showing lush strings of mauve and pink inflorescences.

The grove of olive trees was a less boneheaded feature, and he detoured to the side of the courtyard to have a look at them. They weren't native either, but they didn't hog up scarce water, so it was harder to fault anyone for planting them. They probably had religious significance for these people too, as they were indigenous to Israel. Unfortunately they didn't know how to take care of them—someone needed to pull off all the fruit, and the leaves were peppered with fungal spots. That was easy to prevent if you sprayed for it in the fall but hard to treat once it had taken hold.

"Idiots," he muttered.

Walking into the building through the tall double doors, he was surprised to find it wasn't dark and gothic. There was lots of natural light inside, and it felt airy, devoid of ornate decoration, overall less churchy than he'd expected. At the moment, he saw as he walked toward the back, it was mostly empty, save for a few tourists gawking at the murals, and a pair of women lounging in the pews near the altar.

A couple of watchful people were lurking near the wings, one on either side of the main space, dressed in matching outfits. In another context they'd be bouncers, or enforcers, but here they were probably ushers, or worse, recruiters. One of them was watching Slater, probably ready to make a sales pitch, but the one on the other side, wearing the same black trousers and tan T-shirt with a sketch of the cathedral on the front, looked like she could be Samoan.

Avoiding the gaze of the recruiter on this side, Slater walked away before he could speak, crossing the big room along a row of pews, feigning interest in the murals on the walls high above. They were woven tapestries, he realized, almost photorealistic depictions of a line of people in profile, all of them facing the altar.

Wandering over near the other recruiter, he saw that she was curvy, with her black hair butched short, the image on her T-shirt distorted by her bulky breasts. As expected, he didn't have to approach her; when he got close enough, she spoke to him.

"Are you looking for the confessionals?"

Slater scoffed. "What good would that do?"

"God forgives everyone."

"No thanks," he said lightly.

"I know you're not a tourist."

"I'm just looking the place over. I've never been inside before."

She turned toward the altar and gestured to the high luminous windows. "To me the simplicity of the design is befitting of our city. The architecture reflects the untarnished potential of the newest part of the New World."

"Untarnished? You should come to my neighborhood. But I'll admit it's much less colonial and oppressive than I thought it would be. Lo, modernity."

"That almost sounds like praise."

"The simplicity thing is just because it's cheaper to build that way. If you run everything like it's a business, there's never going to be any extras."

"You're not really a church person, are you," she said.

"So, what, you stand here to recruit people for the confessional booth?"

She laughed. "I'm a docent."

"I thought those were in museums."

"There's lots of art here too."

"I guess you could call it that." Slater eyed the tapestries again, the parade of meek obedient morons. Turning back, he met her eye. "What do you know about Dawn Snowden?"

Her face hardened. "You sick fuck."

"Hey, sister—you're in a church. Nothing makes Jesus angrier than coarse language in his fancy house."

"How many of you has she got on her payroll?"

"I'm not working for that nut job. I thought maybe you were."

Her eyes narrowed. Slater could see the curiosity burning, and the anger. All he had to do was wait for her to ask.

"What's your connection to that hungry ghost?"

"I'm looking into her," he said. "She's blackmailing a client of mine. We haven't been able to come to financial terms."

She scoffed. "Good luck with that."

"Has she got you on the hook?"

"Who the fuck are you?" she demanded. "Is this some kind of game she's playing with me?"

Slater dug in his hip pocket and handed over his business card. "Like I said, I'm looking into her."

"Ibáñez," she said, looking at the card. "Like the guitars."

"No relation."

She glanced across the vast room to where the other docent was standing, openly watching them.

"Come and have a coffee with me."

Slater followed her into the wings and out into the courtyard.

"What's your name, anyway?" he said.

"Etta."

"Are you Samoan?"

"My family is," she said, glancing at him side-long. "Why do you ask?"

"Just curious."

"Well, if the game is guessing my ethnicity, you win. You look Latin."

"I'm more of a mutt."

"Like what?"

"Jewish, and Honduran, although some of my people are in El Salvador."

"If that's the case," Etta said, "You can't tell me you've never been inside a church before."

The courtyard café was quiet, with just a couple of the tables occupied. At the counter inside Slater ordered a soy latte.

The woman at the register shook her head. "We don't have soy milk."

"Of course you don't. Give me a double espresso."

Etta ordered a horchata, and they went out to sit in the courtyard.

"First off, how did you find me?" Etta said, leaning back and eyeing him across the little table.

"I overheard the peroxide number talking about one of her victims. Someone who worked at the cathedral and was Samoan—and here you are."

"I guess that makes sense. What exactly do you want with me?"

"Just your story. I'm trying to figure out the extent of Dawn's trash-bag activities."

Etta nodded, and took a deep breath. "I went to

Dawn's shop to get a couple of photos printed and framed. I asked her if I could email the images. She said, 'Are they on your phone? Just give it to me; it's easier.' She took my phone into the back of her studio. It was just for a couple of minutes."

"She copied more than those photos."

"I never even thought of it." Etta looked down. "It was a video."

"Were you murdering someone?"

"Of course not. I had a sex video. I never should have made it."

"There are a dozen celebrities floating around this town who are famous for nothing more than the fact that they have a sex video. How could Dawn blackmail you with that? It could actually improve your brand."

"I don't have a brand," she said, gesturing with her paper cup. "I work for the church. The cathedral is only a volunteer gig. My paying job is as an educator. I teach at a church middle school."

"The bishops might be celibate, but surely they're not opposed to the rest of the world having sex."

"In the video I was with a woman." Etta jutted her chin a little and held his gaze. Slater recognized that look—her unconscious defiance, aggregated from all the years and all the effort of coming out again and again.

"So what?" he said, and sipped his espresso.

"If my school's administrators saw it, I'd lose my job."

"Because of the gay thing?"

"Exactly."

"That's messed up." Slater waved at the facade of the cathedral. "Why would you work for these degenerates?"

"It's my faith." Etta gestured helplessly. "It's not all bad."

He stifled a sigh of frustration. "Are you sure they can shit-can you just because you're gay?"

"Federal law has religious freedom exemptions. Religious organizations can set their own rules."

"That's totally infuriating. I should probably know about stuff like that, since I'm dick-exclusive."

"You mean you're gay?"

"That's what I just said." Slater folded his arms. "How long has blondie been bleeding you?"

"A few months."

Slater looked away, mulling it over. "I'm going to put an end to it," he said finally.

"Are you talking about croaking her?"

"I'm going to take her down, put her out of business. I won't have to kill anyone. Do you want to help me with that?"

"As long as nobody gets iced," she said carefully, "I would love to help you with that."

Slater pulled out his phone. "My card has my phone number. Give me yours." He punched it in as she rattled it off, then sent her a text with his name. Her phone chirped in her pocket—she'd given him her legit number.

"Do you know who works with her on the grift?" he said, tucking his phone away.

"I've only dealt with Dawn." Her brow furrowed

in thought. "You know, once there was a guy in the shop."

"Young guy, lots of hair, works the counter?"

"I know him too, but this guy seemed to know what was going on."

"Why do you think that?"

"She sent the clerk into the lab in the back, and closed the door on him, but she didn't hide anything from this other guy. I paid her, and he stood right there and watched."

"An employee?" Slater said.

"I don't think he works there. He was hanging around in front of the counter, dressed in a suit."

"Do you know his name?"

"Dawn actually said it. Something Anglo and snappy." Etta frowned. "I have to remember fifty new students' names every fall. Give me a minute— it'll come to me." She screwed her eyes shut for a moment, then opened them again and slapped the table. "Marty."

"You have a great memory. Does Marty have a speech problem?"

Her eyebrows shot up. "You've met him. He sounds exactly like that character in the cartoons. Sylvester the Cat."

FIVE

⌿⌿⌿⌿⌿⌿⌿⌿⌿⌿⌿

DRIVING BACK TO HIS office, the long shadows of the low winter sun were darkening the neighborhood as evening set in. The parking lot was almost empty, and the lobby of his building was deserted.

Upstairs the lights were off, with no sign of Max, and Slater sat at his desk, pulling the keyboard close. A search for "Marty" and "photography" brought up a long list of people and businesses. When he added "lisp," the first entry was an online review:

> Marty was able to convert my old family slides into digital images and correct the color. The photos look natural now. His rates are reasonable considering his level of fame. Marty is personable, and he has an adorable lisp.

The link led to a business-card website for Marty Gregson Photography. It had some airy advertising language about integrity and professionalism, but more significantly, there was a photo of Marty. His hair was reddish-blond, cut in an upscale style, and he had a sharp nose, and dark eyes, with a faint smile on his thick lips. Basically fuckable, Slater decided.

Pulling out his phone, he texted the photo to Etta, and added a message:

Is this the guy?

Her reply came a moment later:

You found him.

Reading more reviews of Marty's business, it sounded like he specialized in converting prints, negatives, and slides to digital format. It lined up with what Dawn had grilled him about. This guy was doing the opposite for her, putting digital images onto old-school rolls of physical film. But Marty was more involved with her than just production—he'd offered to go shake down Etta, for one thing, and if Dawn couldn't afford to pay him, it meant she owed him a lot more than what a simple film job would cost.

The address listed for Marty was on Spring Street. When Slater checked a map, he saw that it was residential, one of those big rental buildings in that neighborhood. Most of them were new construction, capitalizing on the zoning change that allowed people to live in an erstwhile office district. Even though the salespeople called them lofts, they weren't actually office or warehouse conversions, just bland purpose-built apartment buildings like you'd find anywhere.

If that was his business address, it meant Marty worked from home. It was so close to Dawn's studio that the guy would definitely walk there, and on the recording she'd told him exactly when to come back—opening time tomorrow. Slater looked up her business. Opening time for her was eleven.

A plan started to coalesce in his mind. Depending on what kind of person Marty was, it might just work. Picking up his phone, he dialed Etta's number, glad that she picked up.

"Friday is a school day," Slater said. "Why weren't you teaching today?"

"School gets out at three-forty. I volunteer at the cathedral until five."

"I guess that fits."

"Why would I lie about that?" Etta demanded. "You're so suspicious. You can look it up on the school's website. As long as we're being nosy, Friday night is Shabbat. Why aren't you at temple?"

"Why would I do that?" He scoffed. "Listen, are you free tomorrow morning? I have an idea."

He explained the plan he'd formulated, and told her what she'd have to do, and answered some of her questions.

"Right on," Etta said finally, her excitement palpable now. "I love this idea. When should we meet?"

After Slater ended the call, he checked the time. The sun was long gone, although he wouldn't have known that in here—Max's office had the only window, facing the wall of the neighboring building, although if you stood close to the glass you could see a sliver of the sky.

He needed to eat something, he realized, and then sex and booze. Considering the options, he sent a text to Andy:

Are you available for a sleepover?

Andy did some hacking for him sometimes, although he didn't call it that, preferring the term "research." Normally Slater didn't like to hook up with guys more than once, but Andy was different. Part of it was that he did twelve-step. Working the program made him easy to be around—Andy didn't tell him what to do, or make demands, or put expectations on him.

Lately they'd been trying sleepovers. It was a step beyond hooking up, but not a crazy extreme move like declaring exclusivity. It was annoying to be there sometimes, camped in his space, with all his junk, and he kept the place too cold, but the payoff was worth it—he got to sleep with Andy.

His reply came a minute later, and it made Slater smile:

Affirmative, but you have to feed me first.

Slater locked up the office and headed down to his car, then drove the few blocks over to Broadway, where he parked in the surface lot behind Andy's building and paid the attendant the evening rate.

This place was a legit loft conversion, an old cotton warehouse with the original board floors and old-timey multipane windows. When he got upstairs and rapped on his door, it took a moment for him to open it.

Andy greeted him with that easy smile. He had a few days' stubble on his face, and his usual unkempt mop of brown hair. He was dressed to go out, in chinos and an olive-green sweater.

Stepping inside, Slater met his warm mouth, and got lost in it. Andy put a hand on the back of Slater's neck to steady himself, his rhythmic random muscle movements telegraphed through his fingers. Eventually he pulled back.

"No time to … loiter, son," he said. "I'm hungry."

Slater nodded. "Are we scooting, or stick walking?"

It had taken a while for Slater to wrap his head around the idea that "use it or lose it" didn't apply to Andy's musculature, and he'd eventually come to accept the electric scooter he sometimes rode. Still, he much preferred when Andy used his walking sticks, even though he moved slower.

"Sticks it is," Andy said, stepping farther inside and fitting his arms into the cuffs.

Once he was ready, he waved Slater into the hall with one of them. Slater waited while he locked the door. Without much fine-motor coordination, it took him a while, but Slater knew better by now than to offer to help.

Finally Andy dropped his keys in his trouser pocket. "Race you."

Slater grinned at that, and they walked to the elevator, and rode down to the street. A leisurely stroll to the central market, a few blocks away, kept him at Andy's pace. Inside, the place was bustling, with people lined up for the trendy eateries.

"Pizza?" Andy said, and gestured toward the stand with the domed brick oven. They sat on stools at the counter, and he propped his sticks beside him. The counter guy, wearing a red polo shirt and a ball cap, stepped over, and a minute later they'd ordered.

"So is there any … specific reason you called … tonight?" Andy said.

"I couldn't stop imagining you riding my dick."

"That's so mushy and … sentimental. You're making me all … misty-eyed."

Slater shrugged. "The dick wants what the dick wants."

"I thought maybe you were trying to … cock-block me on a Friday night so I wouldn't … sleep with other people."

"It's not about the weekend. Your bed is my second favorite place to sleep."

"I'd come to your … apartment," Andy said, "but it's too depressing."

Before long the counter guy presented their pizzas, and they dug in, and ate in contented silence. Slater noticed the staffer eyeing them, especially Andy. The way he ate probably looked chaotic, and messy, but he got the job done. A minute later the guy stepped over.

"Do you need some more napkins?"

"Keep them coming," Andy said.

Afterward they stopped at one of the few

traditional market stalls still here so that Andy could buy some fruit. Slater carried the bag for him as they walked back to his loft.

His place was one big room plus a bathroom, with a desk near the kitchen counter, his bed, and a couple of easy chairs. The tattersall windows that filled one wall looked out over Pershing Square.

Andy leaned his sticks against the wall next to the little table, then approached Slater, and grasped his shoulders. He had the odor of cooking on him, and a fleck of tomato sauce at the corner of his mouth. Slater pulled him close, reaching under his sweater, running his hands over his warm skin. Andy sank onto the bed, pulling Slater down with him. He swung a knee over Andy's legs to straddle him.

Despite the big talk, Andy wasn't going to be riding him—sex with him actually took careful maneuvering. He pulled off Andy's sweater, then his own shirt, and leaned down to kiss his mouth, massaging his chest. Groping his crotch through his chinos, he found that he was already hard.

Pushing him up, Andy unbuckled his belt. Slater slid down the bed and pulled his chinos off, then sat up to pull off his own boots, and ditched his jeans. With both of them naked, he climbed up and straddled Andy's hips, pressing their cocks together.

Andy grabbed his thighs, rhythmically kneading them. "You have such a great body."

"Someone told me recently I need to go to the gym."

"You don't." He squeezed Slater's cock, eliciting

a sigh. "Do you want to … go down on me?"

"Yeah, I do," he said softly, and ran his fingers into his hair.

"Then let's get to it, punk," Andy said. "Suck my … dick."

Slater chuckled and shifted position so he could rest his forearm across Andy's thighs. No way did he need a black eye from a flailing knee when he had a muscle spasm. Taking him into his mouth, he worked him gently, until Andy's body was vibrating. As he came, he grabbed a handful of Slater's hair and involuntarily yanked at it.

Slater rolled onto his back, and when Andy had caught his breath, he shifted closer, grabbing his cock in his iron grip and stroking him. Slater nuzzled his ear, and smelled the heady scent of the sweat in his hair, and then climaxed, breathing hard.

When his panting had subsided, he got up to grab a towel from the bathroom, and tossed it to Andy, then went to the pantry cupboard. Andy kept a handle of bourbon here for him. It was much better stuff than the applejack version he bought for himself. He uncapped it and poured out half a glass, then slammed it, closing his eyes to relish the vapor in his nose, the burn in his throat. Once he'd rinsed the glass, he took another brief pull from the bottle before he put it back in the cupboard.

After he killed the lights, he climbed into bed with Andy, shifting close to him, luxuriating in the intense warmth of his skin.

"You smell like a distillery," Andy said.

"Thank you," he mumbled. "I feel like a distill-ery."

Wrapping an arm around his wiry frame, he felt the glow in his belly, seeping into his brain. This was the best place he could be right now, warm and content and sated.

———◆———

Daylight was streaming in Andy's big windows when he woke. Alone in bed, he saw that Andy was up and working on his computer, wearing his usual tank top and boxer shorts. Slater watched him for a while, in profile, absorbed in the array of oversize screens. His desk chair was a high-backed curved thing that other people used for gaming, but for Andy it was an adaptation for his CP.

Without looking at him, Andy spoke. "You're staring at me."

"I know you hate that."

"So why do you do it?"

"Maybe it's compelling because it's forbidden. Like drugs."

Andy shot him a look. "So get clean, son."

"You know I'm older than you, right?" Slater rolled out of bed and went to wash up, then pulled on his clothes. Stepping over to Andy's chair, he put his hands on his shoulders. Andy leaned back to kiss him.

"Thanks for … staying over."

"Bye, beautiful."

Walking out to the street, he went around to

the lot where he'd left his car, and climbed in, then found his sunglasses and pulled them on. He didn't usually wear them, unless he was seriously hung over, or the sun was too obnoxious, or he was out in the desert, but he'd need them today, as he was going to be loitering on the street.

His car could stay here, he decided. It was just a couple blocks to where he was meeting Etta, and at this point the attendant was going to charge him for the whole day anyway. He locked the vehicle and strode toward Spring Street.

Even though he was a few minutes early, Etta was already waiting at the corner. That was a good sign—she was committed to this plan.

When she caught sight of him, she waved, and he looked her over as he approached. Gray sweatpants with blotchy stains on the legs, a ratty T-shirt, and a thin nylon jacket with a rip at the shoulder.

"Your outfit is perfect."

"I feel like a slob," she said. "It's scary how easy it was to put together a homeless look from my own wardrobe."

"There's a *tiendita* around the corner."

As they walked toward it, Etta said, "What do we need, exactly?"

"A glass bottle with something colorful in it."

Stepping inside, Slater pushed his sunglasses up into his hair, and they stood together to peruse the drink case.

"Something sticky, like soda?" Etta said.

"Let's use this." Slater pulled out a quart of tomato juice.

Once he'd paid for it, they walked back to where they'd met. There was a coffee place on the corner, and Etta nodded to it.

"Maybe I'll hang out in there. I hope they'll let me, dressed like this."

"Make sure your ringer is on," Slater said, handing her the bag with the juice. "And take the bottle out of the bag. It won't work through the paper."

She frowned. "I get it, Slater. I did two years of drama in college. I think I can handle this."

"Let's hope so."

He turned and walked up the block, until he was a few paces past the front entrance to Marty's building, and stood near the parking meters along the curb. Watching the pedestrians stream by, he remembered his sunglasses, and pulled them down to conceal his eyes.

Dawn's shop opening time came and went, and there was no sign of Marty, even though he kept a close eye on the surprising number of people walking around. Loitering here was getting tedious. At one point a homeless idiot shuffled past, then stopped to look him over. This guy had all the time in the world, he knew. Slater raised his sunglasses to stare him down. The guy was lucid enough to get unnerved, and it wasn't long before he scowled, and turned, and shuffled away.

Slater was starting to wonder if maybe Marty had gone out the back way, or taken his car, or changed his plans. His phone buzzed—Etta.

"No sign of him?" she said.

"Dawn told him to come at opening time. That

was at eleven, but I think we should wait a little longer."

"I'm getting wired. I'm on my third coffee."

"So drink something else. Stakeouts take time."

Slater tucked his phone away and folded his arms, stifling a yawn.

A few minutes later, his heart started to pound when a familiar face stepped out of the apartment building. He was in a teal-blue suit, and his reddish hair glistened in the daylight. There was no mistaking him: it was Marty. Slight and not very tall, he was carrying a little black bag, the size of a clutch. As anticipated, he turned and strode down the block toward Dawn's studio, toward Etta, moving with the idiosyncratic swagger of a short guy.

Digging out his phone, Slater dialed her.

"Headed your way," he said. "Teal suit."

"Yikes," Etta said, then added, "Wait—teal?"

"Greenish blue. Dude is a redhead. He's hard to miss." Slater ended the call. Whatever she taught at that school, it must not involve vocabulary.

Slater let Marty get a dozen yards ahead before he moved to follow him. The street was busy enough that no one would see what he was doing, and Marty would never notice that he had a tail. It was actually a great suit, he saw, watching him walk, cut tight to flatter his wiry frame.

Marty was approaching the corner with the coffeehouse, and Slater walked a little faster when he caught sight of Etta, the tomato-juice bottle dangling from her hand. She was ambling along with her head down, shoulders hunched, moving diagonally across the sidewalk. As Marty came up on her, she veered across his path. The guy tried to sidestep her, but they connected, and the bottle smashed on the concrete with an audible *pop*.

"Damn it," Marty snapped.

Etta started shouting at him. "Oh! You did not just do that to me. Who do you think you are, breaking my stuff? You don't own the damn sidewalk."

"I'm soaked," he shouted. "What is this crap?"

Slater was almost on them. So far it had worked—Marty had engaged with her, and he'd stopped walking.

"You did that on purpose," Etta cried, pointing a finger at him.

"I didn't break your bottle, you big junkie. You did."

"You're going to have to pay for that."

"Calm down, sister," Slater said, his tone authoritative. As he stepped up to them, he kept an eye on Etta but casually placed a hand on Marty's shoulder.

"Oh, hell, no," Etta said, and ramped up the volume, spewing a stream of abuse: "You're a damn assassin. Did your mother teach you to act like this?"

"You got it all over your pants," Slater said, and pulled out a handkerchief, then crouched beside Marty, dabbing at his pant leg.

At the same time Etta lunged toward them, jabbing her finger as she spoke. "It's not his street. You can't come down to my sidewalk in my neighborhood and smash up my stuff."

Marty stepped back, keeping a wary eye on her

but also absently moving away from Slater's handsy attention. Rising, Slater pulled out another hankie, handing the first one to Marty.

Marty frowned and glanced at him. In that moment Etta stepped closer and poked his shoulder.

"Hey—I'm talking to you," she shouted.

"Back off," Marty snapped, and recoiled from her. Without looking, he took the hankie that Slater thrust at him, and Slater bumped his elbow, in the same movement taking the little black bag from under his arm.

"Leave the man alone," Slater said, stepping in front of Marty and waving his arm, as if defending him, holding the bag out of sight against his leg. With his free hand he moved to dab at Marty's crotch with his hankie.

"You don't need to do that," Marty said, brushing his hand away.

"Take this, then," Slater said, and pushed the second hankie into his hand.

Etta lunged at him again in a feint, spurring Marty to step back and hold up a palm. By now other people had stopped to watch, and Slater stepped behind the guy, then turned and walked up the block. Etta continued her histrionics to provide him with cover, and it worked, as no one was looking at him—except one pair of eyes. Slater noticed him in his periphery as he stepped away from the confrontation. A chubby guy dressed in black sweatpants and a black T-shirt. Walking fast, Slater didn't look back.

A moment later the chubby guy caught up

to him, trotting parallel. His shoes were shabby and had wire twisted through the top two eyelets instead of laces. Slater ignored him until the guy spoke.

"Hey—that's not your bag," he said.

Turning to face him, Slater grabbed his wrist and twisted it hard. The guy yelped as he was forced to spin away from him. Slater pushed his wrist up into the middle of his back.

"That hurts," he shouted.

When he caught a whiff of the guy, his instinct was to let go. It was the gnarly tang of homelessness—vinegar and ammonia and rot. But he held firm, and breathed through his mouth, and growled in the guy's ear.

"Shut the fuck up, or I'll dislocate your shoulder."

"OK," he said. "OK."

"Are you going to let it go?"

"Yes."

Slater shoved him away, then walked fast toward the next cross street. As he rounded the corner, he glanced back. The guy was standing there, rubbing his shoulder and watching him go, but no one else was paying any attention.

Farther away, Etta was still shouting, and waving her arms. More people had stopped to gawk. From here he couldn't tell whether Marty was still in the middle of it or not. Hopefully Etta was smart enough to switch it off before it attracted the cops.

It would be faster to head to his office from here than to walk back for his car, so he kept going. When he'd made it another block, he zipped open Marty's bag. Inside were two little yellow cans—the rolls of film for Dawn. The bag also contained a cell phone and a silver clip with Marty's driver's license on one side and a credit card on the other. There were several more plastic cards stacked between them.

"Damn it," he muttered. Stealing the guy's wallet hadn't been part of the plan. Why did Marty keep all this in a handbag? Was that suit cut so tight that it didn't have any pockets?

SIX

A FEW MINUTES LATER, SLATER walked up on his building. For the clothing business Saturday was a regular workday, and he stepped aside to let a guy push a garment rack off the elevator before he boarded. Up in the office there was no sign of Max. He went to his own desk and opened Marty's bag. Eight cards in all, he found, and arranged them on the desktop to photograph them with his phone, then flipped them all over and photographed the backs.

Once he'd shuffled them back together in the silver clip, he checked the guy's cell phone; as expected, it was locked. The little canisters each contained an industrial yellow film container. He could see how it functioned—there was a slit for the strip of film to slide in and out, and gears at the top and bottom to turn the central spindle to wind up the spool of film. The yellow housing was marked 35 MM, and COLOR NEGATIVE, and in big black letters, 100. They were both the same, he saw, turning them over in his palm.

His phone rang, and he pulled it out of his jeans—Etta.

"You got his bag?" she said, her tone hushed. "You didn't even have to go for his pockets."

"The bag made it easy. It has two rolls of film in it."

"Yes," she hissed.

"You did excellent work. He was extremely distracted."

Etta cackled. "I've seen enough crazy in this town. It's not hard to emulate."

"You left before the cops showed up?"

"I left after Marty did. He wasn't there for very long after you took off."

"And he didn't notice he was missing his stuff?"

"He bolted," Etta said. "Your hankie was still in his hand. He couldn't get away fast enough. So what do we do next?"

"I'll get the film developed, and from there we'll know if we can use it against the Aryan capo."

"How are you going to do that?"

"I'll figure it out. Give me a day or two."

"It feels good to be doing something," Etta said. "Taking action, you know?"

"I know. We'll get them," Slater said, and ended the call.

As he set his phone down, Marty's phone buzzed on the desktop. His first instinct had been just to bust it in half and toss it, but he decided to pick up.

"Who's this?" Slater said.

"I've got a better one for you." It was Marty's voice. "You're answering my phone. Who the hell is this?"

"I'm glad you called," Slater said, affecting an amiable tone. "I found this little black bag on Spring Street."

"Was my wallet in it?"

"No, there's no wallet, but there's a silver clip with a stack of bank cards, and a driver's license on top."

"Hallelujah. Was there anything else?"

"That's all I found," Slater said, and pulled open his top drawer, dropping the film canisters inside. "The phone and the cards and the little black bag. It was zipped half open, so I'm surprised there was anything inside. I was going to drop it off at the police station."

"Don't do that. Where are you? I'll come and pick it up."

"I'm out doing stuff, but I'm not far from where I found it. Can you meet me at the coffee place on Spring?"

Slater ended the call and then wiped his prints off the phone. Once he'd zipped it into the little black bag with Marty's cards, he killed the lights and locked up the office, then went downstairs and walked back to Spring Street.

Marty was waiting on the corner, his red hair visible from half a block away, but he'd ditched that great suit for cargo pants and a polo shirt. Stepping up to him, Slater flashed a smile and handed him the bag.

"That's definitely your photo on the driver's license."

Marty's eyes narrowed. "I remember you. You were there. When the crazy woman broke her bottle."

"She seemed to think you broke it."

"You tried to wipe off my suit."

Slater shrugged. "I felt sorry for you."

Marty studied his face, his brow furrowing. Slater could see the wheels turning as he scoured his memory.

"Did I hand you this bag?" he said finally.

"I found it on the street right over there," he said, gesturing vaguely behind him. "I think you were already gone. I didn't know whose it was."

"Did you see some little yellow cans?" He held his thumb and finger a few inches apart. "About this big."

"All that I found was the bag and the phone and the cards."

He sighed. "Well, I'm glad you brought them back."

"You're wearing different clothes," Slater said. "I felt bad about that beautiful suit."

"I live right there," Marty said, gesturing to the towering apartment building up the block. "I went home to change. That's when I realized I didn't have my phone." His eyes narrowed, as if he'd suddenly remembered something, and he zipped open the bag. Pulling the cards out of the silver clip, he shuffled through them. "I think they're all here."

"I understand why you lost them," Slater said. "You looked a little traumatized."

"There's more Skid Row types around here every day. I don't usually get attacked, but when you live here it's impossible to avoid them."

"Do you know that little bar on the next corner?" Slater said. "Let me buy you a drink."

He frowned. "It's the middle of the day."

"It's Saturday."

Marty hesitated, but then waggled his phone. "It's rare to meet an honest man. Sure, you can buy me a drink."

Slater feigned a nonchalant smile and waved the way across the street.

As they walked toward the place, Marty eyed him sidelong. "What's your name, anyway?"

"John Slade."

"I'm Marty, although you knew that already if you looked at my ID."

The bar was surprisingly busy for early afternoon, and they sat at the only open stools at the counter. The bartender, a harried-looking woman with her hair bundled on her head, stepped over, and Marty ordered a small of pale ale.

"Same for me," Slater said, and dug out a twenty, setting it on the bar top. Slater was the one who'd helped him out—it would make more sense if Marty were buying.

The bartender set down their beer glasses and plucked the twenty.

"Sweetheart," Marty called to her, holding his drink up to the light. He waited for her to turn back. "Can you at least give me a clean glass?"

Without a word she took it from him, and returned a moment later with another, along with Slater's change. At least Marty had the manners to clink his glass on Slater's before he drank.

After he'd taken a sip, Slater eyed him. "So what do you do for a living, Marty?"

"I'm LA's premier photographer."

From the look on his face, he was dead serious.

"That's quite an achievement. You do head shots for actors?"

He frowned and waved dismissively. "Those hacks are a dime a dozen. I'm a professional. If you followed the art world, you'd know I've had gallery shows of my work on both coasts. My photographs hang in the best museums on three continents."

"Impressive. Do you have a studio?"

"I don't need a studio. People come to me. I'm in high demand."

Slater sipped his beer and looked him over. If that were true, why did he need to work for Dawn? The way Marty was leaning over the bar, he saw that even though he was slight, he had a little flab over his belt.

"You're in good shape. Do you work out?"

"I don't, but I have good genes," Marty said. "And that sounds like a pickup line."

"It could be, if you're into it."

He flashed a thin smile. "I get this a lot. I know I'm attractive, but I just don't swing that way."

Slater scoffed. "I can't even count the number of straight guys who were a couple tequila shots away from swinging that way."

"You're confident, I'll give you that."

"It's your loss."

Marty gulped at his beer. "It's all just genitals anyway."

"You're not interested in genitals?"

"I see a lot of them. I dabble in adult entertainment." He waved a hand. "In production, not as an actor—although of course I could, obviously."

"Obviously," Slater said. "I can't imagine sex as a job. It would take the fun out of it."

"It's lucrative, though. It amazes me what people are willing to pay to see other people's junk, and what other people are willing to pay to keep their sex lives secret. But whatever—I'll take their money."

The guy wasn't talking specifics, but Slater knew what he meant—he was being totally blithe about extorting people like Etta.

"It sounds like a racket," Slater said.

"Just capitalism. Like a tax on stupidity." He drank from his glass. "What do you do, anyway?"

"I'm in insurance."

"You don't look like a white-collar guy."

"Yeah, it's pretty boring." Slater drained his glass and slid off his stool. "Last chance—I'll smoke you in the men's room, right now."

"No thank you," Marty said firmly.

"Hang on to that," he said, gesturing to his little black bag, then headed for the street.

———·———

BACK IN HIS OFFICE, Slater did another web search for Marty. In addition to the listing for his photo business that he'd seen earlier, there were a few reviews of his technical work, and a listing on a website that seemed to be an aggregator of pages about fine art. It contained some black-and-white photos of twisted-up driftwood that were attributed to Marty Gregson, but he couldn't find any mention of gallery shows.

In his pants his phone buzzed, and he pulled it out. It was a notification from the audio bug in Dawn's office. He clicked on the recording and heard her voice, but there was no one else talking— she was on a phone call.

"You were supposed to bring them today," she said. "How could you just lose them? It's only a few minutes' walk."

Slater sat up to listen. She was talking to Marty.

"Just make another roll, then … It probably doesn't matter. Anyone who decides to develop those won't know who the subjects are … Not yet … You'll get paid when I get paid. Morales is dragging his feet. I know he's not having trouble raising the money. Maybe *go's* people have deeper pockets … Tonight at the Baltimore … I'll bill them both. The worst-case scenario is that neither of them pays, and I'll have to publish. But I'm thinking they're both going to pony up … No, I'm going to get a room there, so I can have the film nearby if he brings cash. I don't want to carry it around on me … Well, you'd better hustle, then. I need it by closing time."

The recording ended, and Slater stared absently

at his phone as the backlight faded out. This was incredibly tantalizing—Dawn was meeting another victim at the Baltimore Hotel tonight. "*Go's* people," whatever that meant. He knew exactly how he could find out.

Picking up his phone, he scrolled through his contacts and found Miguel, a guy he'd hooked up with once. He'd kept in touch with him because he worked at the Baltimore, and it was useful to have a contact in a place like that. Slater sent him a text:

Are you at work today? Can I see you?

His reply came a moment later:

Just got here. Working the swing shift. Ask for me at the staff desk.

Slater was across the street before he remembered his car wasn't here—it was still at Andy's. As luck would have it, the Baltimore was just across the square from that lot, and he set off, walking through the Fashion District and into the Historic Core.

The Baltimore was a block-long grande dame of a hotel, and the lobby and bar and public spaces upstairs bore the grandeur of the early twentieth century. Slater went around to the alley and into the staff entrance. Down here they'd spared the ornamentation—the ceiling was claustrophobically low, the paint was peeling, and exposed pipes ran along the wall.

Behind the staff desk, wedged in a room with no doors, really just a wide spot in a hallway, was a fresh-faced woman wearing the hotel's uniform:

a white shirt with a burgundy vest. Her name tag said VERA. Slater asked for Miguel, and she picked up the phone, murmuring into it. A minute later Miguel stepped into the space, dressed the same way Vera was. He was in his thirties, and dark, and had a belly, a little heavier even than the last time Slater had seen him. His hair was precisely groomed and smooth with pomade.

Miguel greeted him and beckoned him to follow, walking deeper into the bowels of the hotel.

"You look sharp," Slater said, walking behind him.

"And you look like my wet dreams."

Miguel stepped into a room lined with dark-green lockers and a pair of benches in the middle. No one else was inside, and Miguel closed the door behind them.

"I assume you need a favor," he said quietly.

"I want to hire you to help me out. I have a lead on a meeting here tonight."

"There's a wedding scheduled in one of the ballrooms. Is it that? I'll be working it."

"This is just two people," Slater said. "I think it must be happening in the bar."

"That makes sense. The lobby is too busy to talk privately."

"I want to get close enough to overhear them, so I need a reason to move around the bar. Maybe I could borrow your vest and bus tables."

Miguel nodded. "I can arrange that. I'll tell the bar staff you're a G-man or something. But it's going to cost you."

"It always does. How much to use your clothes for a couple hours?"

"I don't want cash this time."

Slater frowned. "What do you want?"

"A date."

"Like dinner and dancing?" Slater scoffed. "No way. You can slap me around and fuck me, but no dates."

"Good god, man, I don't want to brutalize you."

He waved impatiently. "I just mean I'll do any sex thing you want, but not a weekend at a bed-and-breakfast in Ojai, or a long walk on the beach, or whatever it is that civilians do."

Miguel sighed. "You're a complicated man."

"Actually, I work hard to keep things simple."

"Fine—it's a deal. When is your meeting?"

Slater thought about that. Dawn had told Marty to bring her the film by closing time.

"Sometime after eight. One of the targets works until then."

"So you'll come back." Miguel looked him up and down. "I'll find a uniform that'll fit you before that. Text me when you get here."

Slater found his way out to the alley, then headed across the square toward his car. The sun was low in the sky, almost gone for the day. He dug out his phone and went through his contact list, trying to remember the name of the guy he needed to talk to. It jumped out as he scrolled past it—Jack.

When he dialed, a man's voice answered. "Urban Hair Events."

"I'm looking for Jack," Slater said, pausing at

the street corner to wait for the crossing signal. "I thought this was his cell."

"You sound interesting. When did we hook up?"

"The name is Slater. It was a few months ago. How do you know we hooked up?"

"Jack is a nickname. I only use it for gentleman callers. My real name is John."

"I know your other real name is Miss Mercy Daze."

The light changed, and Slater followed the cluster of pedestrians across the street.

"That's more a stage name. Not much about her is real."

"Well, I want to hire her."

"Ooh, darlin', she's ready. Do you need an MC? I have a mike and an amp but no turntables, so you'll need someone else to do the music."

"It's not an event. I need to look older."

"It's a makeup job?" Jack said. "Sure, I can do that. It's not nearly as much fun as performing, though."

"The deal is, it has to be today. The sooner the better."

"There's a surcharge for rush service."

"Whatever it takes," Slater said.

"You can drop by my studio. I'm here now. I'll text you the address."

Once he'd paid the parking attendant, Slater climbed into the Thunderbird and put Jack's address into the navigation app on his phone. It was in Los Feliz, he saw, and headed toward the freeway.

SEVEN

THERE WERE CLUBS AND eateries on this strip, Slater knew, cruising up Vermont, and they got busy on Saturday evening. It took a few minutes to find a street space to park the Thunderbird. Walking up on Jack's address, he saw that the doorway was next to an old-school restaurant, one of those places that had been here forever.

A pair of box planters with horsetail in them stood on either side of the entrance, a blatant attempt to update the postwar vibe. Designers usually put that stuff in front of Asian-themed joints because it looked like bamboo, but it was no less knuckleheaded to plant it in front of an Italian restaurant. It looked trendy, and it grew well in limited space, but it was a water hog.

The door to Jack's place was unlocked, and when he pulled it open, he found a flight of stairs leading up. The odor of grilled food and tomato sauce got stronger as he ascended to the landing at the top. There were three doors up here, likely three apartments above the eatery. Jack had said it was unit B, and he knocked on that one.

When he opened the door, Jack cracked a smile. "I remember you."

His dark hair was slicked back, and he had on a tight black T-shirt and an indigo-dyed wraparound sarong. Jack's jaw bore a trace of stubble, and he was wearing subtle eye makeup, and maybe lip gloss.

"Come on in," he said, and stepped aside. "We had fun that time, didn't we?"

"That's how I remember it."

It was a studio apartment, and there were clothes everywhere—loaded onto a pair of sagging garment racks, stacked on the credenza, strewn on the sofa. Slater wanted to ask if he was moving, but this was probably Jack's baseline. At least there were big windows to open it up, with the twilight outside fading to evening.

"This is the makeup area," Jack said, pointing out the little round kitchen table with a pair of folding chairs. The tabletop was obscured by a bulky aluminum box that was folded open to reveal layers of trays laden with brushes and jars and little boxes of colored powder.

"You're serious about this stuff," Slater said.

"Have a seat."

Once he'd taken a chair, Jack sat too, and shifted closer, until their knees were almost touching, and studied his face.

"What exactly do you need?"

"Like I said, to look older. It needs to look real—not exaggerated like glam drag."

"Slater needs to pass."

"Exactly."

"Why? That's so boring," Jack said flatly. "Who do you have to fool?"

"That's confidential."

"I thought you were an insurance salesman."

"Insurance investigator. You don't need to know the why. You're a professional, right? Just do the damn work."

"Fine," he said flatly. "What are the lighting conditions going to be?"

"It's in a bar, so I'd say not very bright. I'll be serving drinks to someone I've met a couple times. I don't want her to recognize me."

"So it's not just older," he said, and furrowed his brow. "You need to look like a different person."

"Can you do that?"

"Of course I can. My dilemma is whether it's ethical."

Slater frowned. "That makes no sense."

"It seems sad to make you look old," he said, and rose to dig in the makeup case. "Are you sure you don't want me to make you into a femme fatale instead? You'd look very different. Unrecognizable."

"I don't think I can pass as a woman. I don't really know the body language."

"That would definitely draw attention."

"Like a chimp on a unicycle," Slater said. "I need to fade into the background."

"You've never done drag?"

"I wore guy-liner in high school."

"That doesn't count." Jack sighed. "Fine—we'll make you look older. I'll have to sell you a wig rather than loan it to you, because I'll have to cut the hair."

"How much for the whole makeover?"

"Including the rush surcharge," Jack said, "let's say two fifty."

Slater nodded. "I can do that."

Jack walked behind the clothes racks and returned a moment later with a black-and-gray wig.

"First we'll get the hair right, and then I'll do the makeup."

"You just had that lying around?"

"Of course."

Jack stood behind him and pulled the wig onto Slater's head, adjusting it and tucking away his real hair. It was less uncomfortable than he'd expected. Grabbing a pair of scissors, Jack went to work snipping at it. It felt just like getting a real haircut.

Moving in front of him, he put a finger under Slater's chin, tilting his head up, then to the sides. Apparently satisfied, he snatched the wig off and dropped it on the table.

"You need a shave," Jack said, and went through a doorway, and flicked on the room light.

As he brushed the hair off his shoulders, Slater could see a shower curtain inside, tucked into the side of a bathtub. When he returned, Jack had a mug in one hand and a straight razor in the other.

"With that?" Slater demanded. "No freaking way."

Jack set the mug on the table. "It's the best way

to get the skin smooth enough to act as a proper base for the makeup." He put one hand on his hip, and raised an eyebrow, and flipped the razor open. "Don't you trust me, stud?"

"Of course I don't."

"It's totally safe. What are you afraid of?"

"You could murder me, or have a seizure and do a Van Gogh on my ear."

"I have a cosmetology license," Jack said. "Although—full disclosure—it's only valid in Florida. Come on. It'll take thirty seconds."

Slater clicked his tongue and leaned back in the chair. "If I don't make it, my car is parked in a two-hour zone on Vermont. The keys are in my front pocket. It's a black T-bird."

Jack scoffed and swirled the brush in the mug, working up a lather. Next he wiped Slater's face with a warm wet cloth, then applied the soap.

"Hold very still."

Slater closed his eyes so that he wouldn't flinch. The blade moved over his jaw and his neck, and soon Jack was wiping off the residual foam with a cloth.

"Damn, that's close," Slater said, feeling his cheek.

"You've never had a real shave before?"

"I guess not."

"Next is wrinkles," Jack said, and pulled a little tub out of his makeup case.

"Do you make any money doing this?"

"No talking while I'm working." He stepped closer and tapped under his chin. "Head back."

Slater tilted his chin up and closed his eyes again.

"This might feel a little weird, but hold still."

It felt gummy, whatever he was applying at the corners of his eyes, and below them, and at the sides of his mouth.

"It should dry pretty quickly," Jack said.

Slater spoke through clenched teeth, not wanting to disturb his work. "It smells like acetone."

Next he felt soft dabbing on his face and neck, like a sponge, and then brushes, and then something finer, like the point of a pencil. Jack chatted as he worked, a rambling monologue about his makeup career. He'd done some work in the entertainment industry, and he talked about the celebrities he'd worked on. Slater hadn't heard of any of them.

"I always do camera-ready makeup," Jack explained. "That means news shows and reality television. They want people to look natural, but with no makeup at all, the camera makes you look like a corpse."

Rummaging in his makeup case, he produced what looked like a gray caterpillar.

"The mustache will seal the deal," he said. "I'm going to glue it on. You can't move your mouth for a couple minutes."

The chemical he painted on his upper lip smelled worse than the acetone. Jack fanned it for a moment with his fingers, then pressed the band of gray hair onto it.

"Once the smell is gone, it's dry."

"How do I get it off again?" Slater said through his teeth.

"Hot water. That thing is high-end. It should move with your skin like real hair." A minute later, he said, "That should be long enough. Try moving your lip."

Slater bared his teeth and then pursed his lips.

"Nice," Jack said. "Very natural."

Next he pulled the wig back onto Slater's head, then wet his hands at the kitchen sink and squeezed some hair gel into his palm. He ran his hands into the wig, and spent a minute adjusting it.

"I think you're ready," he said, and gave Slater a hand mirror.

"Fuck me," Slater said, taking it in. He looked decades older, wizened and gray.

"Any time, cowboy."

"The wrinkles are the same color as my skin."

"They have the same makeup on them."

"What are they made of?"

Jack shrugged. "Some kind of plastic. You can peel it off in the shower."

Handing the mirror back, he met his gaze. "I knew you'd ace this."

"How? You've never seen me in drag."

"Even as a guy, you're well put together."

He preened a little at the compliment. "Just don't touch your face, or rub your eyes, or scratch your hair, or you'll ruin it."

"Got it."

"If you really want to sell it, make your eyes look bored. People won't even look at you."

"Show me," Slater said.

"Like this." His eyes went soft, his expression

blank. "Just think of nothing, or something boring, like memorizing numbers."

Slater tried it, relaxing his vision and staring into space.

"Excellent." Jack clapped his hands. "I wouldn't look twice at that weary old mug."

Rising, Slater pulled out his wad of cash and counted out three C-notes.

"We said two fifty," Jack said. "I don't have any change."

"It's a bonus for your high level of skill."

Jack thanked him, then followed him to the door. "Have fun tonight, whatever it is you're up to."

Downstairs, as he walked past the cluster of smokers hanging around outside the restaurant, no one seemed to notice him, even though a couple of them glanced his way. That was an excellent sign—despite the weird sensation of the wrinkle makeup and the wig on his scalp, it meant he looked nondescript.

As he climbed into the Thunderbird, he saw that there was an alert on his phone from the bug in Dawn's office. He put the phone on speaker and pulled into the traffic. It was Dawn's voice, but no one else's—she was on a phone call again. He listened for a minute to her talking about printing a photo, and the size of it, and how to crop it. That was her legitimate business, he decided—not the grift. He didn't need to hear it. Slater tapped the phone to stop the playback.

On the way downtown, he wanted to touch his face, scratch an itch, but he forced himself to resist.

Whatever Jack had put on his skin wasn't really that uncomfortable, but it was maddening not to be able to touch it. This was going to be a long evening.

Slater nosed the vehicle into the garage under the square, then as he walked across to the Baltimore and headed for the alley entrance, he texted Miguel. The guy was already standing near the staff desk, gazing at his phone, when Slater walked up. Miguel glanced up at him, then looked back at his screen, but then did a double-take, his eyes narrowing as he studied Slater's face.

"*Vato*, seriously? You look like my old man."

"Good."

Miguel led him back to the changing room and pulled open one of the green lockers.

"These should fit you," he said, pulling out a pair of black trousers, a white shirt, and a burgundy vest—the uniform the staffers wore.

Slater sat on the bench to pull off his boots, then his jeans.

"Who did the disguise?" Miguel said, watching him step into the pants.

"A friend who does drag."

"You look really different. As long as the person you're spying on doesn't look too closely, you'll be fine."

The pants fit pretty well, and he buttoned the dress shirt, then pulled on the vest.

"Arnold?" Slater said, reading the gold name tag pinned to it.

"He's off today. You're lucky he's your size."

"I'll need a pass key for the guest rooms," he

said, pulling on his boots. "And my target is staying here tonight—I'll need her room number."

Miguel groaned. "You didn't tell me that part. I could get in serious trouble."

"So I'll throw in some cash along with the pony ride," he said, and grabbed his own crotch.

"I'll need a grand."

"Six hundred," Slater said, "plus all this." He gestured to his torso.

Miguel didn't hesitate. "Deal." He dug in his front pocket and produced a small white card, the size of a bank card but thicker, and handed it over. "This will open any guest room."

"Can it be traced to you?"

"Totally, but I can delete the records for it after you leave tonight. What's the guest's name?"

"It'll be under either Dawn Snowden or Dawn Strezlecki."

"Christ, what is it with white people's names?" He pulled out his cell phone and handed it over. "Write it down for me."

Slater thumb-typed the names, then handed it back.

"Wait here," Miguel said, and went out to the hallway, closing the door behind him.

There was a mirror in the corner, and Slater stepped over to it, adjusting his shirt collar and the black clip-on bow tie. The shades of makeup that Jack had used were close to his own coloring, and he'd done a great job—he couldn't detect the point on his neck where the makeup ended.

Miguel stepped back inside and closed the

door. "That name is booked in room 707, but the guest hasn't checked in yet."

"Excellent."

"Listen—if you get caught, you've never heard of me. You found the key card on the floor."

"I'm not going to get caught."

Miguel nodded. "I talked to the bartender. He knows the skinny. Just tell him who you want to eavesdrop on, and he'll help you make it look natural."

"There's just one bartender?"

"Plus someone doing table service. Weekends aren't busy here. We mostly get business travelers."

"Do I need to cut him in?"

"He didn't ask for that, but maybe you could leave a Benjamin in the tip jar or something." He waved an arm. "Come on—I'll introduce you."

Upstairs, Miguel led him through the back entrance into the bar. The public part of it was tony, with dark wood paneling and elegant stonework. Apart from the bartender, the only other person in the room was a patron on a stool at the end of the bar, absorbed in his phone.

"This is Isidro," Miguel said. "He's running the show." The bartender stepped toward them and flashed a polished smile. The guy was rotund, in his fifties maybe, and had slick dark hair. His black vest showed his status as a notch higher than the rest of the staffers in their burgundy. After Slater introduced himself, Miguel clapped him on the shoulder.

"Call me if you need me," he said, and left.

"So what's your experience with bartending?" Isidro said.

"I don't really know how to mix drinks, but I can run the well and the beer taps, and I can clean up."

He nodded. "That's good enough. When you're wearing the uniform, it looks better if you're not just loitering."

"So give me something to do."

Isidro handed him a white cloth. "This is linen. It puts a nice shine on the glasses after they've been machine washed. You can work through this tray."

"I appreciate you letting me be here."

He shrugged. "If Miguel says you're OK, you're OK."

Slater started polishing glasses and scanned the empty room. There were a dozen tables arranged in the space, all of them visible from the bar. It was warm in here, he realized, and his head was itching under his wig.

A woman appeared from the public hallway, wearing the same burgundy vest as he was, her black hair pulled into a tight knot behind her head. She approached the service area of the bar. Slater was close enough to read her name plate: RENATA. She shot him a quizzical look, and he greeted her with a nod.

Isidro stepped up to talk to her, and filled a couple of glasses from the beer taps. She carried them over to a table where a straight couple was just sitting down. They were dressed formally, the guy in a dark suit and the woman in a long dress, maybe headed to the wedding Miguel had mentioned.

Another trio wandered in and occupied a table, keeping Renata busy for a few minutes. There was no sign of Dawn, but the busier it got, the easier it would be to eavesdrop on her.

EIGHT

s SLATER STOOD THERE working on the glasses, things were picking up, with more of the seats occupied. A couple of guys walked in and sat at a table near the bar. One of them looked like a bodybuilder, and his dress shirt was way too tight, revealing his nipples. But if he had those pecs himself, Slater reasoned, he'd want to show them off too.

Renata was at another table, and the muscle-head looked around, then got up and approached the bar, catching Slater's eye.

"Two tequila shots and two IPAs," he said, and pulled out a credit card.

"I'll bring them over," Slater said. "You can pay then."

The guy left, and Slater found the tap for the IPA, and filled two glasses. He'd never done this, but he'd seen it done often enough to know he had to tilt the glass so it wouldn't get too much head on it.

Isidro had his hands full, mixing a string of drinks farther down the bar, so Slater found the shot glasses and filled a couple from the tequila bottle in the well, then set them with the beer in the service area.

When Renata returned, she quickly loaded them onto a tray. "Who are these for?" she asked him.

"The guy with the rack." Slater nodded toward the muscle-head.

She frowned and glanced in that direction. "Which guy?"

"Are you blind? He's stacked." Slater jabbed a finger toward them. "Blue shirt, spray tan, big pecs. He ordered but he hasn't paid."

Renata grinned and eyed his name plate. "That's table 9, for future reference. Thanks, Arnold."

Even though the place was half full now, the bar work slowed down for a while, and Isidro was able to keep up without Slater's help. He found the rolling rack for the empties parked in the back, and moved some of the stuff that Renata had bused onto it, then polished more beer glasses.

It felt like it was getting late, and there was no sign of Dawn. He'd be pissed if she didn't even show after he'd gone to all this trouble—a whole evening where he wasn't able to touch his own face.

A cut for Isidro and Renata, he remembered, eyeing the tip jar. It was a brandy snifter on the bar, near the service area, and contained a few crumpled singles and coins. Miguel had told him to put some cash in it for them. He should do it now—once Dawn appeared he'd likely forget all about it. Digging in his pants pocket, he peeled off two C-notes and folded them up, and palmed them, then tucked them under the singles in the glass.

A man's voice rose over the lounge music, and Slater looked out at the room to see Renata beside a table with a patron sitting alone. He was a skinny guy with pockmarked skin and a dark suit. Slater couldn't hear her side of it from here, but he could tell that it wasn't her who was escalating things; she was speaking to him calmly. He glanced at Isidro. He was tuned in to it as well, watching them closely.

"Come on, man," Isidro said, almost under his breath. "Don't do it."

The guy at the table raised his voice again and slapped Renata's arm.

"That's it," Isidro said. "I'm calling security."

"Do you want me to eighty-six the guy?" Slater said.

Isidro eyed him. "It's better if I get a security guard."

"It'll be quicker if I do it."

Stepping around the bar, Slater approached the table. Renata was flushed.

"Step back," he told her, and as she did, Slater grabbed the guy by the collar and pulled him out of his chair. He was taller than he'd expected, but he was clearly inebriated, and unsteady on his feet.

He tried to shrug Slater off and pull away. "Let go of me."

Slater held firm. "If you'll come with me."

The guy turned and took a swing at him. It was sloppy enough that Slater was able to grab his wrist in mid-lurch and twist his arm behind his back. He yelped in pain, and Slater frog-marched him out into the wide hallway. Every eye in the bar was on the disturbance, watching him—this hadn't been part of the plan, drawing this kind of attention to himself.

"Dude," the drunk said. "Let go. Quit being a bully."

"Shut the fuck up," Slater growled, and steered him toward the front of the hotel.

Halfway to the lobby, a guy in a security guard's jacket caught up to them.

"Tell him to let me go," the drunk said.

The guard ignored that, and spoke to Slater. "You got him?"

"Where am I taking him?" Slater said.

"Not into the lobby. There's a side door to the street." He pointed ahead of them. "Right up there."

The guard trotted ahead of them and pushed the crash bar to open the door, then held it wide. Slater hustled the guy up to it, and when he reached the threshold, gave him a hard shove and released his grip. The drunk stumbled across the sidewalk and landed on his butt, on the rim of a concrete planter that enclosed a ratty ficus tree.

The guy stood up and steadied himself against the gnarled trunk, then jabbed a finger at Slater. "Fuck you."

"No thanks," Slater said. "You're too loaded."

"Don't come back in here," the guard said,

raising his voice, "or I'll arrest you." He put a hand on Slater's shoulder and drew him back inside, then pulled the door closed. "It's risky to take that on by yourself. Drunks can be unpredictable."

"I knew I could handle him," Slater said, stepping away from the door.

"Do you have security training?"

"Middle-school wrestling, and street brawling."

"Next time, wait for one of the guards. At your age you should know better. You could break something."

"Will do," he said, suppressing a smile, and turned to walk back to the bar.

In here the eviction was already forgotten. Isidro was chatting with a pair of miniskirt-clad women perched on barstools, his expression animated, and Renata was over at a table delivering highballs. Slater picked up the linen cloth again and grabbed a beer glass from the clean tray.

In his pants his phone buzzed, and he pulled it out to check. It was a text from Miguel:

> Your target just checked in. No change in the room number.

Miguel was really earning his pay tonight—and Dawn was here.

Renata approached the service area, and Slater stepped over.

"Thanks for taking out the trash," she said.

"My pleasure."

"I need two smalls of the hefeweizen and a soda water, for table 30."

Slater held up a beer glass. "A small is this size?"

Her eyes narrowed. "Correct."

She stood waiting, so he hustled to find the right tap. Once he'd poured the beer, he filled a highball glass with soda water from the fountain, and set it on her tray.

"You need to put a lime wedge on the water."

Turning around, he surveyed the array of supplies until he found one, then pressed it onto the glass.

"Are you new, Arnold?" she said.

"First day."

She grinned and lifted the tray.

"What did you just give Renata?" Isidro said, stepping over.

"Two small hefeweizen, one soda water, table 30."

As Isidro punched it into the register, Slater caught sight of Dawn, walking in from the hallway. She was wearing a short powder-blue skirt and a little white jacket.

He spoke under his breath. "That's my target."

"She's a looker," Isidro said, watching her approach. "Gams for days."

"Don't look too close. It's all poison under the peroxide."

"You want to wait on her?"

"I won't need to go near her until her friend shows up."

Isidro went to the far end of the bar, where Dawn had perched on a stool. Slater kept his head down, polishing a glass, but tuned in to their conversation.

"A Manhattan petite," Dawn said, her tone perfunctory, disinterested, avoiding eye contact.

Isidro turned to the array of bottles behind the bar. Slater could see her in his periphery, the puff of dried-out blond hair, but she didn't even glance in his direction.

Once she had her drink, and signed for it with her room key, a guy walked in, clearly looking for someone. In his forties, he had slick black hair, and his luxy gray suit looked tailored. Spotting Dawn, he walked over, and greeted her, and sat on the adjacent stool. They knew each other, Slater saw, but they weren't friends. The guy stretched his arm on the bar top, revealing his chunky wristwatch. That looked expensive—he was a high roller, or wanted people to think he was.

He wished he could photograph this guy, but it just wasn't safe to try—someone would notice. Walking past Isidro, he stood facing the shelves of bottles behind the bar, with his back to Dawn and the man, close enough to overhear them.

"That's way too much," the guy was saying. "I'm not made of money."

"That's not what the pictures say," Dawn said.

"I'm not even in those pictures. I doubt you could pin it on me."

Slater couldn't just stand here motionless, so he reached up and pulled a bottle from the shelf, and set it on the counter in front of him.

"Morales would flip in a hot minute if the cops put the screws to him," Dawn said. "You know he would. That would put you firmly under the bus."

Cinzano rosso, Slater saw, looking at the bottle. He screwed the cap off and poured a couple fingers into a tumbler.

"I need to talk to my partners," the guy said. "I'm not sure if we can come up with that kind of money."

"Oh, you'll do it," Dawn said. "If I don't hear from you by Tuesday, the DA will hear all about the pictures."

Slater turned to face them, just long enough to get a better look at the guy's face. It was risky, but neither one of them even glanced at him. Carrying the tumbler of Cinzano, he went into the back. It seemed a waste to just leave it on the rack of empties, so he slammed it before he set down the glass, enjoying the sweet mellow flavor. He strode to the service elevator and punched the button for 7.

Something didn't fit, he thought, on the ride up. Dawn had mentioned Morales by name, but it seemed like she was trying to extort the guy in the shiny suit for the same photos. And why would the DA care about photos of Morales with some woman? Clearly there was more to it.

Stepping off the elevator, he strode the hall until he found room 707, then dug out Miguel's key card and tapped it against the lock. The light on the lock turned green, and the bolt retracted. He took a breath. *Thank you, Miguel.*

Pushing the door open, he called, "Housekeeping."

There was no answer, and the room was dark. He closed the door softly and hit the light switch.

It was a narrow space, with a small window, but the bed looked plush. Nothing had been touched since the cleaners had been here, it seemed. The only evidence of occupancy was a bulky black handbag on the end of the bed.

Slater pulled it open and quickly dug through it. A ring of keys, tampons, a tin of mints—but no film. Dawn had definitely said she wanted to leave the film in her room while she met with her mark. Glancing around the space, there were dozens of places she could have hidden it. He looked in the bedside table, then in the desk drawer, but he didn't have time to ransack the place—Dawn's meeting had already been winding up when he'd left the bar.

Poking his head in the bathroom, he saw there was a makeup kit on the sink. He zipped it open and hurriedly went through the contents—tubes and little containers and pencils. The sweat was pooling under his wig; he could feel it. Dawn might be here any second.

There was a bulge in the soft lining of the case, he saw, and when he felt it, the size and shape were definitely right for a film canister. There was an outside pocket, and he zipped it open. A smile spread across his face. It was the same canister as the ones he'd taxed from Marty—a yellow container with a spindle and marked with a big 100.

Zipping the bag closed, he pocketed the film and hustled to the door, killing the lights before he let himself out. Walking to the elevator, once he was away from Dawn's room, he took a deep breath.

He'd gone the wrong way, he realized—these

were the guest elevators, not the ones for the staff. At this point it didn't matter if he drew attention to himself, he decided, and punched the call button. Waiting for the doors to open, he sent Miguel a terse text:

Finished.

The elevator paused on the floor below to let people board—a gray-haired guy in a sport coat, and with a hand on his arm, a surgeried woman with an immaculate coiffure and a spray of glittery jewelry. As they stepped on, both avoided his gaze. It was revealing to see how people didn't even acknowledge the help, as if he were an invisible part of the infrastructure, like the carpet or the chairs or the ducts inside the walls.

Down on the staff floor, Slater found the changing room, and the locker where he'd left his clothes, and started to get undressed.

Miguel appeared and closed the door behind him. "How did it go?"

"I learned what I needed to." He handed him the card key. "I only used it once, to get into 707. You'll delete the access record?"

"That's my next stop."

It made sense that he was incentivized to do it, Slater thought, eyeing him as he pocketed the card. It was his own key—if Dawn complained about something missing from her room, it would implicate him.

"Why do they even keep track if you can just delete it?" Slater said.

"Ideally the people who handle security would be separate from the people who work in the rooms. But for a publicly traded company, profit is the prime directive, so you start cutting back on staff, and doubling up on responsibilities, and paying people starvation wages."

"And corporate America gets hoist with its own petard."

"So—about our date," Miguel said, watching Slater step into his jeans.

"It's not a date."

"How about tonight? I'm off in an hour."

"Come by my place," Slater said. "I'll have your four dollars."

"We settled on six, you lousy crook."

Slater grinned as he buttoned his shirt. "Is that what we said?"

"Maybe I will smack you around."

He shrugged. "Dealer's choice."

"And maybe don't wash off the old-man look just yet."

"Seriously? It's itchy as hell."

"It's kind of hot," Miguel said. "Let's experiment with it."

"Then don't be late," he said, and walked out.

The cold night air felt good as Slater stepped out into the alley, and he hustled across the street against the light, then down into the garage under the square. As he drove out of downtown, across the 110 freeway toward his neighborhood, he wanted nothing more than to rip the itchy rug off his head. But he didn't—wearing it a little longer was part of the cost of doing business with Miguel.

Once he was up in his apartment, he pulled off his boots and stretched out in his recliner. There was good music on Saturday night, and he turned on the radio, and closed his eyes, and sank into the rhythm.

A sharp knock roused him, and he got up to open the door. Miguel was in his civvies now, chinos and a collared shirt, his hair still immaculate.

"It's so weird to see you so much older," Miguel said, a wry smile on his face.

"What are you going to do about it?" Slater demanded, holding the door wider for him to step inside.

Once he'd flipped the deadbolt, Slater stepped closer to him. Miguel put his hands on his waist and met his mouth. It tasted minty. This guy was so well organized he'd even prepped for kissing him. Slater broke away and ran his hands into his lush hair, and mouthed his jaw, and his ear, and his neck, eliciting a heavy sigh. He put his palm on Miguel's back and steered him toward his bedroom.

As he unbuttoned his shirt, Miguel jutted his chin at him. "Are you going to show me who's boss, old man?"

"I can do that."

Slater took off his own shirt, then ditched his jeans. When he stepped closer, Miguel squeezed his cock, already half hard. Unbuttoning Miguel's chinos, Slater slid them down, then straightened up and slapped his face.

Miguel put his hand on his cheek. He looked startled.

"Too much?" Slater said.

"Not that kind of boss. Just fuck me like you're the boss."

He pushed Miguel onto the bed, then straddled him, and massaged his chest. Makeup was smeared around his mouth, transferred from Slater's face.

"Who's your daddy?" Slater said.

Miguel giggled and pulled him closer, and mouthed his neck. Shifting beside him on the futon, Slater worked a finger into him, then another, and then reached to the bedside table for a condom and lube. Rolling it on himself, he kissed Miguel again, lingering in it, then penetrated him. Grabbing his calves, Slater started to pound him as Miguel groaned, his face contorted. But the guy was into it, his eyes bright. Slater held his gaze for a moment, then arched his back and climaxed.

Breathing hard, Slater rolled onto his side. Miguel turned toward him, his hand on his own cock, and nibbled at Slater's jaw. Slater massaged his chest, then met his mouth and forced his tongue inside. A moment later, Miguel pulled away and gasped as he came.

Slater yanked off his wig and threw it in a corner of the room, then closed his eyes, catching his breath.

"I can taste whatever's on your face," Miguel said.

"A whole bunch of makeup."

"Can I shower?"

"Knock yourself out."

Slater heard the water start, and then he drifted

off, waking again when Miguel returned.

"From the nose up you still look elderly," he said, looking Slater over, "but from the nose down you look like you were motorboating a mole enchilada."

"I guess I should shower too."

Miguel pulled on his underpants as Slater sat up. "You're not going to hang out?"

"I have to take my kids to early mass tomorrow," Miguel said, snatching his shirt off the floor.

Slater's eyes narrowed. Who knew the guy had that kind of family. "Of course. It's Sunday."

He found his jeans and dug in the front pocket for his wad of cash, then peeled off six C-notes, part of the bundle he'd taken from Morales, and handed them over.

"Sweet, sweet cash," Miguel said, beaming as he tucked them away.

After he'd left, Slater locked the front door, then went into the bathroom. His own face in the mirror startled him—Jack's makeup job was completely messed up. It took a minute to peel off the rubbery wrinkles around his eyes. It was weird stuff, but it had looked authentic—no one had questioned his appearance, or even glanced at him twice.

Once he'd showered off the makeup residue, he went into the kitchen, and cracked open a fifth of bourbon, and poured out his ration. It was supposed to be savored, of course, but his purpose was to achieve an end, so he treated it like applejack. He slammed his ration, then poured another inch or so, and killed the lights, and stretched out in his recliner.

The amber liquid warmed his belly and started to seep into his mind, making him smile. Eyeing the dark roofline of the building across the street, he knew he wasn't going to be conscious for long. That didn't seem right—he was too wiped out even to enjoy the buzz.

NINE

As SLATER WOKE, SLOWLY coming to consciousness, he realized he was in his own bed, and his head didn't hurt. Scrabbling for his phone on the bedside table, he checked the call log, relieved that he hadn't phoned anyone overnight. That was a good sign—part of his revised booze rules, the thing about rationing his intake, was to put an end to drunk-dialing people.

There were three rolls of film now, from Marty's bag and the one Dawn had brought to sell to the guy in the bar. He needed to get them developed today. Max would know how to make that happen, and like Slater, he couldn't afford to take Sunday off. He sent him a text:

In the office today?

His reply came a moment later:

Here now, until about noon.

Slater climbed out of bed and went to wash up, then pulled open the fridge. There was nothing to eat, but he took out the jar of powdered coffee and dumped a few spoonfuls into a mug, then filled it from the tap and put it in the microwave. A minute later, once he was dressed, he grabbed the mug and gulped at the lukewarm ersatz java, wondering whether he should wear a jacket. Fuck it, he decided. How cold could it get? He dumped the brown dregs in the sink, then went down to his garage and drove to his office.

The clothing factories were closed on Sunday, and the building looked deserted as he crossed the street from the parking lot. Upstairs, as he stepped into the office, he saw Max's gray suit jacket hanging on the coat rack next to the front desk.

Max was parked behind his own desk, wearing a rumpled white shirt and a yellow necktie. His sidearm and its holster sat on the desktop. He glanced up but didn't say anything, as he was listening to his cell phone, pressed to his ear and almost completely concealed in his meaty paw. Slater waved and went into his own office.

As he settled into his desk, he could hear Max's side of the call.

"It's possible he did it himself," he said. "Sometimes a muscle spasm can send the weapon some distance."

What the hell was he working on? Max did a lot of couple disputes, window-shade jobs where people wanted evidence that their spouses were cheating, but this one sounded gruesome.

A sharp knock at the door roused him from his thoughts. Slater got up and pulled Max's door closed, then went to open the front door. It was Dawn, her straw-dry blond hair tied back, wearing jeans and a white top that was sheer and billowy and totally inappropriate for winter. She was scowling at him.

"I don't know how you did it," she said, "but I know you did it."

"You seem upset," Slater said.

"Of course I'm upset, you moron." She huffed and waved an arm. "Are we going to talk about this in the hallway?"

Slater stepped back, opening the door wider, and made a sweeping gesture. "Would madam like to come in?"

As he closed the door, Dawn eyed the statue of Rey Pascual.

"Is that the drug cartel mascot?"

"Not even close."

"So why is a skeleton wearing a crown?"

"Because he's the king of the graveyard."

"That seems kind of threatening in a place of business."

Slater walked into his office, around behind the desk, and dropped into his chair. "That's the second time you've accused me of threatening you. It makes me think you're like a hydrangea in the heat."

"What the hell does that mean?"

"You're too sensitive."

She scoffed at that, and he gestured to the chair in front of his desk, but Dawn ignored it, and stood there as she glanced around his office. Slater reclined and interlaced his fingers behind his head.

"Why so agitated, princess? Did someone put a dent in your pink Corvette?"

"This place is a dump."

"Thank you. So what is it that you think I did?"

"You ripped me off."

Slater gestured helplessly. "I don't know what you're talking about. I'm waiting for my client to raise the funds for you, but he's having trouble. It's a lot of scratch."

"Spare me the sob story. Morales has more cash tucked away than you'll ever see in your lifetime."

"How do you know that?"

"Because I'm the one with the pictures," she said, raising her voice.

That didn't really make sense, Slater thought, watching her talk. "What exactly do you think was stolen from you?"

"Don't even try to lie about it," she said. "You know exactly what it was. I came to tell you that I keep digital copies—safe from thieves."

"You know that Morales is a powerful guy, right? He's head of the planning and land-use committee. I'm told they basically decide what happens in this town. Are you sure you want to extort him? He could make you disappear."

"And I could burn him to the ground in a heartbeat," she said, shouting now. "And you too, you penny-ante thug. So don't fuck with me."

"I'm not a thug," Slater said flatly. "If you want a representative sample of that type, you should look in the mirror sometime."

Dawn jabbed a finger at him. "If you think you can steal from me, trust me—it'll cost you."

Slater sat up and took a breath. "I guess we'll see."

Dawn whirled around, and stopped short at the sight of Max, standing in his office doorway, hands on his hips. His holster was on now, with the butt of his weapon visible. Regaining her nerve, Dawn tossed her hair and marched to the front door, slamming it behind her.

"I did not expect to see her today," Slater said, stepping into the front office.

"It sounded like she was getting aggressive," Max said. "I figured maybe seeing someone was armed might calm the waters."

"Good call."

"Is she part of your blackmail case?"

"She's the grifter," Slater said, and followed him into his office. He sat in front of Max's desk and told him about Dawn, and stalking her at the bar in the Baltimore, and rifling her hotel room.

Max waved a hand. "How did she figure out it was you that pinched the roll of film?"

"I don't think she did. I suspect she's taking a stab at all the likely culprits, throwing her weight around, trying to stay in control of the situation. I knew she'd have other copies, but I want to get a look at the images, and find out what Morales isn't telling me."

"Why does she use actual film? It's easier not to mess with that stuff anymore."

"She says the physical film makes her product more personal, more tangible."

Max chuckled. "An artisanal grifter."

"I need to get the film developed. Have you got someone who can do that quietly?"

"Her name is Olivia. She's competent and discreet."

"What more could I ask for?"

"Let me call her." Max sat up and pulled out his phone. After a brief conversation, he eyed Slater. "Is it negative film or slide film?"

"On the can it says 'color print film.'"

Max repeated that, then listened for a moment. "It's not an issue. He'll pay you. If not, you can come to me."

Once Max had ended the call, Slater frowned. "Is she worried that I'll stiff her?"

"She wanted to know if she should get the cash up front."

"That's what I would do."

"She said you can go over there now. Olivia has a little lab space in the back of her mother's furniture store. It's right on the edge of Boyle Heights."

"Excellent," Slater said, and rose. "Text me the address."

Back at his own desk, he retrieved the little yellow canisters he'd taxed from Marty, and tucked them into his pocket with the one he'd found in Dawn's makeup kit.

Downstairs, he crossed the street and climbed into the Thunderbird. Boyle Heights was just over the river, and navigating to the address Max had sent, he found the furniture store and its faded sign on a busy boulevard.

Slater parked at the curb and walked up to the place. It looked closed, with no windows to the street and steel bars on the door. When he pulled on the handle, it was locked. Next to the entrance was a little unmarked doorbell. He pressed it and waited.

A minute later the door swung open to reveal a curvy woman, wearing jeans and a sweater, her long black hair tied back. She had subtle eyeliner, and pale skin, but some of that might be makeup.

"Slater?" she said.

"You must be Olivia."

She flashed a smile. "Come on in."

She led him through the retail shop, a big room crowded with sofas and credenzas and easy chairs. It looked like used stuff, with narrow paths among the clusters. The place wasn't really closed—at the side of the space a woman was making a sales pitch to a guy about a pair of chairs, and farther back was a double door to the alley, hanging wide open. Two guys were maneuvering a dining table through it.

"Is this stuff vintage?" Slater said.

"Mostly. Some of the pieces are reproductions. Are you in the market?"

"Just curious."

"It's my mother's business, but I help out sometimes."

She led him into a windowless room at the back. Inside was a big double sink, and a photo enlarger on the counter next to it, and a rack laden with gear—chemical bottles and jugs, a stack of those trays for developing prints, and other equipment. Incongruously, a small microwave oven sat on a shelf at one side.

"What have you got for me?" Olivia said, closing the door and turning to face him.

Slater handed her the rolls of film.

"Do you need prints, or just the negatives?"

"I'm not sure yet. Can I look at them first?"

"This is standard film. I'll charge you sixty to develop them, and you can decide about prints after that."

"Sixty each?"

She grinned. "For all three. You can pick them up tomorrow."

"No way. This is a sensitive job—I can't let them out of my sight."

"Max works that way sometimes too. You want me to do it now?"

"How long will it take?"

"Not long. It'll cost you more—a hundred for the trio."

"I can do that."

"You have to stand by the door," Olivia said, "and keep out of my way."

Slater stepped over to the doorway and stood with his back to it, hands on his hips.

"Don't you need to black out the room?"

"If you need to watch," she said, "I can't very well turn out the lights, now, can I?"

From the equipment rack she pulled down a black bag, made of what looked like velvet or heavy fleece, and then a squat metal can with a black lid.

"I have to feed the film onto this," Olivia said, opening the can and pulling out a metal spool with a spiral frame at either end. "It keeps it from touching itself so that the chemical bath gets to it evenly."

"The can is for the chemical bath?"

"Right. It's called a tank."

She tucked the tank and its lid inside the bag with one of the rolls of film he'd given her, then zipped it shut and folded a velcro flap over the zipper. There was a small opening on either side, taut with elastic, he saw, watching her wriggle her hands into them.

"Technically I'm working in the dark," she said, and stared absently at the wall as she manipulated the objects inside the bag.

A minute later she unzipped it and pulled out the tank, with its lid on now, and tossed the empty yellow film canister into a trash bin in the corner.

"Now the chemical baths."

Olivia ran an inch of water into a glass baking dish and put it in the microwave.

"Why do you need hot water?"

"The chemicals have to be warm."

Once she'd pulled the dish out of the oven, she set the film tank in the water, and then set a funnel in the opening at the top. From the rack of supplies she took a dark-brown gallon jug and poured in enough to fill the container. She lifted the tank and momentarily inverted it, then set it back in the water. Next she grabbed the kitchen timer that sat on the counter and cranked the dial.

"Eight minutes," she said. "Let's see if I can get both the other spools loaded in that amount of time."

Slater folded his arms and watched as Olivia tucked another tank and another roll of film into the black bag, then thrust her hands inside to load the film onto the spool.

Both rolls were in tanks well before the timer rang. She put the second tank into the warm water, then dumped the chemical from the first tank into the second, and filled the third from the brown jug. Another chemical got poured into the first tank, and she reset the timer.

Eventually Olivia opened one of the tanks and lifted out the spool, holding it up to the light. From Slater's vantage point the film looked orangey-brown.

"There are definitely good images on this roll," she said, and put it in a tray in the sink, then turned on the tap and left it running.

"Sometimes there aren't?" Slater said.

"People make mistakes. They set the camera wrong, and everything's underexposed or overexposed. These look right. I'll rinse them for a few minutes, and they're done."

The timer rang and she opened the next tank, holding the film up to the light.

"These look good too," she said, but when she opened the last tank, she frowned. "This one's a shredder."

"What's wrong with it?"

"No images, see?"

Olivia pulled the film off the spool, and even from where he stood, Slater could see it was blank.

"Did it accidentally get exposed to the light?" he said.

"Look at the top and bottom edges. The frame numbers and the manufacturer's info are all clear. That means there was no light leakage. There were never any images on this film."

"Could it be the thing you said about the camera being set up wrong?"

"I don't think so." Olivia held the strip up to the light and pulled it through her hand. "There are no frame edges, no shadows, nothing. I'd say it never went through a camera."

Slater took it and looked at it himself. The sour smell of the chemical bath was still detectable. Olivia was right: there was nothing on this. He balled up the curly brown strip and tossed it in the trash.

"How do I get a good look at the images on the other rolls without making prints?"

"I can print them all in actual size on photo paper," Olivia said. "That's called a contact sheet. Or I can scan them digitally. Software converts them from negatives to normal images."

"Can I do that myself?"

"You'll need a piece of tech called a negative scanner. It connects to your computer."

"Where can I get my hands on one of those?" Slater said.

"I have an old one that I could sell you. It's slow, but you've only got forty-eight frames to scan, so it won't matter."

"How much do you want for it?"

Olivia turned off the tap and pursed her lips. "Three hundred," she said finally.

"You have it here?"

"At my desk. In the next room."

She pulled one of the rolls of film off its spool and ran it through a hand tool that looked like a pair of tongs. It had rubber blades, he saw—a squeegee, to remove the water. Next she coiled it up and put it in a little black can. After she'd wiped down the second roll, she handed both to Slater.

"You should let them dry some more unrolled. The canister is just to transport them."

Slater tucked them into his pocket and then pulled out his wad of cash, peeling off four C-notes and handing them over.

"Excellent," Olivia said, smiling as she pocketed the cash.

She led Slater out and into the next room, where there was a desk with an oversize computer monitor, and a flat-bed scanner, and some other inscrutable electronics. From the floor she picked up a black box, about the size of a desk phone, with a power cord and computer cable coiled on top.

"It's easy enough to figure out," she said. "It has the software built in. Just feed the film into it, and it'll do the rest."

"You've been very helpful," Slater said, tucking the machine under his arm.

"I'm happy to get the work. I don't see Max that much anymore since he went digital."

"You used to do his window-shade photos?"

"I haven't heard it called that before, but that's exactly what it was. Cheating cheaters and their bed games. Speaking of which—are you single?"

"I only do guys," Slater said, and frowned.

She shrugged. "I had to ask."

TEN

WHEN SLATER GOT BACK to the office, the lights were off, and Max was gone. He set the negative scanner on his desk and plugged it in, then connected it to his computer. Soon he had it running, and fed one of the rolls of film into the slot. The machine slowly pulled it through, its internal mechanism making a soft high-pitched whine, and eventually the first photo popped up on his screen. It took him a moment to parse what he was looking at.

In the image, two men stood facing each other. One of them was Morales, but he'd never seen the other guy. He was in his fifties, maybe, and Anglo, and wearing a dark suit without a tie. His hair was graying and he had a bit of a paunch. Behind Morales was a row of urinals, and the space behind the other guy was out of focus, but it looked like a long sink and a hand dryer. They were in a public restroom.

The photo had been taken from waist level, so maybe the photographer had hidden the camera in a briefcase or a handbag. They seemed to be talking, but there was no woman in this image, no sex, nothing blackmail-worthy—unless simply meeting with this guy was somehow scandalous.

The scanner clicked and whirred, advancing the strip of film, and the next photo popped up. This one was juicier: the guy facing Morales had a bundle in hand—a stack of cash, folded in half and bound with a blue elastic. It was exactly like the wad Morales had given him.

In the next photo the guy was dropping the cash into a black shopping bag with a department store logo on it, and in the next image, the black bag was in Morales's hand.

Slater sat back, staring at the screen. This whole case had nothing to do with a woman or an illicit affair. Morales had refused to show him the photo Dawn sent him because he didn't want Slater to know what was really going on—that he'd taken cash from this guy. It made sense that they were in the men's room. That was the only public place you could be sure there were no cameras.

But someone had brought a camera to this meeting. Whoever had taken these photos had to be a confidante of Morales or the other guy. How had Dawn acquired these?

As he watched, more photos appeared. In one image, half a dozen bundles of cash were visible in the shopping bag. The photos had obviously been arranged in sequence to tell the story of a payoff, and it definitely looked like Morales was the one on the receiving end.

The scanner went quiet, and Slater saw that the full roll of negatives had been spit out the back, coiled on his desktop. He threaded the other roll into the machine and waited for the first image.

This was from a public restroom too, but with a different view—a toilet stall, seen from above. Standing inside was a woman in a formal dress, wearing jewelry around her neck, her brown hair styled to tumble on her shoulders. When the next image popped up, a man was in the stall with her, the door closed. He had dark hair and was wearing a black suit and a bow tie.

The overhead camera angle made it hard to identify either one of them, but the next photo that came up bore a clear image of her face. The guy was mouthing her neck, and she'd turned her chin upward, eyes closed, her expression a picture of ecstasy. In the subsequent image her skirt was hiked up, and his pants were around his knees—they were having sex. The series of photos that followed was graphic, a furtive hookup caught on film, and again it felt like the sequence had been arranged deliberately—it included a clear shot of each of their faces, making it easy to identify them both.

Slater thought about it as the roll slowly advanced through the scanner. These two were dressed formally, likely for an event like a wedding. And these shots hadn't been taken by a person—the overhead angle meant it had to be from a fixed camera.

Once the roll was completely scanned and the machine went silent, Slater clicked through the images again and found photos with a clear view of the faces—one of the guy who'd paid Morales, and then one each of the pair in the restroom stall. He cropped them tightly around their heads, so there was no indication of where they were or what they were doing. Next he moved all the images into his cloud storage, then dug out his phone.

In his contact list he found Etta. When she picked up, he could hear music in the background.

"Are you around today?" Slater said. "I want to show you something."

"I'm at Grand Park." Etta raised her voice over the music. "There's a really great band."

"Meet me at the coffee place in the park. I'll be there in a few minutes."

"Could you make it in half an hour? The band is still on."

"Of course—I wouldn't want to interrupt your afternoon of leisure."

"Thanks, man," Etta said, and ended the call.

Slater checked the screen to make sure she'd really hung up on him. Either she was drinking, or just not very perceptive—she hadn't detected his sarcasm.

Grabbing the coiling rolls of negatives, he heaved his boots up onto the desk and held one of the strips up to the light. It looked brown and orange, and there were numbers under each frame. In negative, it was almost impossible to tell what was in the images. The wads of cash glowed purple and black in one frame, and Morales and the man with him had white dots for eyes. What was the payoff about? He needed to find out who this guy was.

Sitting up, Slater rolled up the film and tucked it into his pants pocket, not bothering with the little containers Olivia had given him. After he locked up the office, he went down to his car, and drove to Grand Park.

Despite the concert there was lots of room in the massive garage underneath it, and after he parked, Slater walked up a stairwell into the daylight. It felt warmer here, and the plantings in the narrow urban space always made him feel calmer. They'd been done right—mostly local flora and species that were appropriate to the climate, designed to complement the open spaces. There was some lawn here, but that was inevitable in a place that hosted events with crowds.

At the other end of the park he could see the bandstand stood empty, and the audience was dispersing. As he walked up on the coffee place, he found Etta standing outside it. When she caught sight of him she flashed a big smile.

"How are you, man?"

"Are you high or something?"

"You're so dark." She waved her arm. "I just saw a great band. I'm high on life."

"I guess music can do that. Do you want a coffee?"

Etta nodded and followed him inside. "Get me an iced cappuccino."

"It's freaking winter," Slater said, but ordered it anyway, along with his soy latte.

Once they'd picked up the cups, they went outside into the light and found a bright pink park bench, and sat together, facing the fountain. It was shaped like a flying saucer and had a big shallow wading pool in front of it. Even though it was too cold for wet feet, several kids were playing around the edge of the water, splashing and chasing each other.

"I had so much fun derailing Marty yesterday," Etta said.

"You're a natural. You could go to work for the Nigerian syndicate."

"What do they do?"

"Stuff like what we did. They're also pickpockets, and run slip-and-fall scams."

"I don't think I'll be signing up for that."

Slater pulled out his phone and showed her the cropped photo of the guy who'd been with Morales.

"Do you know this man?"

"I've never seen him before," she said, briefly studying the screen.

"How about these chumps?" He swiped to the cropped faces of the man and the woman in the restroom stall.

"Nope," she said, and handed the phone back. "They were on the film you got from Marty?"

"Correct."

"Those are close-ups—did you edit out the sex? Are they Dawn's other victims?"

"I think so, yeah."

Etta sipped her coffee. "So what's the plan to shut down that ice princess?"

"If I can identify these people, it might give me something to work with. When are you due to make a payment?"

"I was supposed to see Dawn this weekend. I told her she'd have to wait a few days. I was hoping you'd make some progress before that."

"I will," Slater said. "Keep stalling her."

"What about Marty?"

"I actually talked to him for a minute."

"How did that happen?"

Slater explained about finding Marty's phone in the little black bag, and returning it to him. "There's definitely something wrong with that guy."

"Besides the fact that he's working with a blackmailer?" Etta said.

"Lots of people are full of themselves, but with this guy it's like his ego doesn't fit into reality. He's got an ordinary body but he thinks he's irresistibly attractive. He says he's famous, but there's nothing about him online."

"That sounds like a personality disorder."

"Good to know," he said. "Maybe we can use that."

Etta gestured with her cup. "I want to do something besides wait. Something like running that scam on Marty."

"I cook my own pigeons," Slater said flatly.

"What does that mean?"

"It means I work alone."

"You needed my help yesterday."

"Sure, and I might need you again."

She sighed. "Marty and the albino are the pigeons in this analogy?"

"Correct."

"So let's charbroil those fuckers."

A woman was watching them, Slater realized, although she was trying not to be obvious about it, standing near the entrance to the coffee place. She had long black hair and wore jeans and a baggy sweater.

"Do you know her?" Slater said, gesturing with his chin.

"That's Safiya. My girlfriend."

"That explains why she's eyeballing us." Slater looked her over. "You do all right. She's good-looking."

"I know," Etta said, "although I'm not into objectifying women."

Slater waved his arm. "I should have said, from over here it looks like she has a warm personality, and a pure heart, and a sterling moral compass."

Etta got up. "Did anyone ever tell you that you're a handful?"

"All the time."

"Later, Slater."

She walked over to her girlfriend, and Slater watched as she looped an arm around her waist. Draining his coffee, he rose and headed for the stairwell into the parking garage.

He wasn't sure why, but he didn't mind Etta. She'd proved more than competent in running that game on Marty, and she wasn't too proud to pose as homeless for a few hours. More significantly, unlike most people, she went light on the bullshit.

———•———

ONCE HE WAS IN his car, Slater was surprised he had a cell signal underground. He spent a minute checking the location of his idiot ex-boyfriend, Conrad. Back when they were still together he'd managed to put a tracker on the moron's phone. It wasn't just idle curiosity—he needed to keep track of the guy. He was a cop and had access to resources that Slater needed.

The dot on the map showed that Conrad was at home, out in the ass end of the valley, probably parked on his couch playing video games. When he dialed, Conrad picked up.

"So does your department use facial recognition technology?" Slater said.

"Officially, no."

"What about unofficially?"

"Think about it—it's already on your phone to organize the photos of your cousins, and on social media sites to figure out who you are and sell you more stuff. So yes, we have access to similar tech."

"How hard is it to run a photo through that software?"

"The beauty of unofficial systems is that they're not tracked or monitored. It's easy."

"Can I send you a couple photos?"

"Who is it?" Conrad said.

"If I knew that, I wouldn't need you to look it up in a database."

"You know what I mean."

He huffed impatiently. "I'm doing a favor for Doris. Someone is hassling an old friend of hers. The people in the photos are involved in it somehow."

"Fine—I can take a look. Send them over."

Slater knew that angle would work with him, as Conrad had a soft spot for Doris. At some point the two of them had started to conspire behind Slater's back, gossiping about his sobriety, planning who knows what to mess with him, trip him up, make him do stuff he didn't want to do. But at least he was ready for it. The beauty of revealing the Doris connection to this case was that it wasn't a distortion. If idiot Conrad asked Doris about it, she'd confirm Slater's story.

"If you're working tomorrow, can you do it then?" Slater said.

"How do you know I'm not working now?"

"You never sound relaxed when you're at work," he said, thinking quickly. "You sound chill right now. I just figured you were at home, playing your stupid video games, or balls-deep in some sweaty twinkie."

"That's a good deduction. It's almost like you know what you're doing as an investigator."

"It's called physical evidence. The guys you take home are so skanky, I can smell them from here."

"I know you know all about skanky guys," Conrad said. "Listen, I'm not working today, but I'll have someone who's on duty run your photos."

"There's three of them. Call me when you get something."

"The customary response is 'thank you.' As in, 'Thank you, Conrad, for helping me.'"

"You haven't done anything yet, you big mook. Let's see what you come up with."

Slater ended the call and huffed in frustration. Such a freaking idiot, and so demanding. Tapping at his phone, he texted Conrad the head shots.

Cruising up the ramp out of the garage and into the daylight, he drove the few blocks to Andy's loft and parked in the lot behind his building. Upstairs, he knocked on his door.

"You're lucky I'm ... home," Andy said, pulling it open. He was wearing a white tank top and paisley-print boxer shorts.

"You're usually home." Slater closed the door and followed him inside.

"I know why you don't ... text me first," Andy said. "You want to catch me with another guy."

"Like cupcake Kyle?"

"You call him that because he ... looks like a snack?"

"Because he's a little slip of a thing and looks sweet," Slater said, "but when you're done with him you feel nauseous. How is sex with him, anyway? He looks like he might be a bit delicate. The type who bruises easily. Do you know that story about the princess and the pea?"

"I'm not going to talk about him." Andy stepped close and put his hands on Slater's hips, telegraphing his random muscle movements. "I will say, however, he's not ... nearly as intuitive as you are."

"That's not a word I hear very often."

"Physically, I mean. Not in … any other sense."

Slater ran his hands over Andy's biceps. "So Kyle is a cold fish. He just lies there and demands attention."

He chuckled. "That's not … what I said."

"Is he one of those guys who soaks in ice water first, and then wants you to treat him like a corpse?"

"Have you actually met people like that?"

"Only Kyle."

"Stop it," Andy said, and moved closer, and met Slater's lips.

He spent a minute lost in Andy's taut mouth, exploring it, then pulled back. Andy adjusted his crotch and dropped into his desk chair.

"Are you here to get fucked?"

"We can do that, if you want," Slater said. "But I came about work."

"Let's save it, then. I'm going out soon."

"With dirtbag Kyle? Does he always play the corpse, or does he sometimes get you to do it?"

"Not that you're jealous or anything," Andy said. "Because why … would you be? I'm not your boyfriend."

"I'm not jealous. Where are you going with him? Some swanky cocktail bar, where a shot of tequila costs forty bucks?"

"I'm going to see my … mother in Newport. Alone. And Kyle's not a dirtbag. He has solid … values and comes from a prominent family. " He waved an arm. "But he's not you."

"Lucky for him."

"What exactly do you need … me to do?"

"Look into someone," Slater said. "I'll text you her names."

"She has more than one?"

"There's her legal name, and then she works under an alias."

"That's so sneaky."

"I can't judge her for having a pseudonym. LA is purpose-built for reinventing yourself." Slater tapped at his phone. "She runs a photography business, and I already know about her criminal record, so don't worry about that. I need to know what other stuff she might be up to."

"I can do some digging. It's going to cost you."

"It always does."

"So send me the details, and … get the hell out of my place. I need to get ready. My mother … has certain standards around hygiene and dinner attire."

Slater grinned and leaned in to kiss him. "Bye, beautiful."

In the hallway, he paused to finish texting him Dawn's other name, and the address of her business. A minute later he was on the street, and walked around the corner to his car, then drove toward the freeway.

One of Doris's trees had looked like it needed fertilizing, and there was enough daylight left to do it. Soon he was off the 110 and cruising into hilly Mount Washington. Pulling into her driveway, he scowled at the sight of her stupid boyfriend's stupid Boxster, parked next to her Buick. Freaking Albert. So far that numbskull hadn't done anything deleterious to Doris, besides sucking up the oxygen in her house, and eating her food, and drinking her booze, but if he ever did, that was going to be it for Albert.

Opening the trunk of the Thunderbird, he pulled out a bag of fertilizer that he'd thrown in a week ago with this task in mind, then gently closed the lid again. If he was stealthy, maybe he wouldn't have to look at stupid Albert's stupid face.

He lifted the bag onto his shoulder and went around to the side gate and into the backyard, closing it quietly behind him. Once he'd set down the fertilizer near the avocado tree, he went to the garden shed to pull on a pair of work gloves and grab a trowel, and a bottle of barbecue starter fluid, and a box of matches.

In a fallow bed a few yards from the fence, he positioned his back to the house and dropped to his knees, then dug a small hole. Next he took the rolls of negatives from his pants pocket and dropped them in, and doused them with starter fluid, and lit a match. The film caught fire with a *woof,* and feeling the heat on his face, he watched the plastic melt and shrink, consumed by the flames.

Behind him he heard the back door to the house open, then Doris's voice.

"What are you burning?"

Slater rose and turned to face her. "Evidence."

She folded her arms, her brow furrowing. "Should I ask?"

"I wouldn't."

"So what happened with Bud?"

Slater stepped closer to her. "I met the black-mailer. I'm currently looking for a way to shut her down."

"It's a woman?" Doris said.

"An ex-con. Tough as nails."

"Well, whatever you can do, I'm sure Bud will be grateful."

Slater nodded, then met her eye. "Is he an honest man?"

"You mean in his career?"

"Every other week there's some political skulduggery uncovered in this town." He waved a hand. "Sleaze and graft and corruption."

"I never heard that about Bud. When we worked together, he didn't act shady."

"But that was, like, a hundred years ago."

She smiled. "Not quite. But you're right—I haven't been close to him in a long time."

At that moment Albert came outside, and stood on the back step. Literally looking down on him, the guy obviously wanted to make the point that he was here, and there was nothing Slater could do about it. His stupid gray mutton chops were bushier than ever, and he grinned like a lunatic as he called out a greeting.

"Hey, Slater, how's it going?"

"What happened to your face?" Slater demanded.

Albert absently touched his cheek. "I'm growing out my sideburns."

"Aren't you a little old to be having a midlife crisis?"

"Slater," Doris said sharply. "R-E-D, remember?"

It was from one of the parade of shrinks she'd hauled him to in his youth, a technique to avoid offending people. It stood for *rebuff, engage, or disengage,* and of course she wanted him to politely "engage." What she didn't realize was that it wasn't just a reaction—Slater actively wanted to "rebuff" Albert, or more precisely, to smack that stupid look off his face.

"I just need to fertilize the avocado," Slater said. "Then I'll get out of your hair."

Slater turned and knelt again to shovel earth over the gooey remnants of the burned negatives, then rose and went over to the bag of fertilizer, pulling one end of it open. Were the pair of them actually going to stand there and watch him work?

"You brought more?" Albert said. "There's already a bag of fertilizer in the shed."

"It's the wrong kind. Stone fruit needs low-nitrogen enrichment. This is mostly carbonized straw." He dropped to his knees and pulled out a handful, then scattered it around the base of the tree. "It's like in your trade—if someone has a sore elbow, you don't amputate their leg." He paused to give Albert the once-over. "Although maybe you would."

"I'm not that kind of surgeon. I do knees. And that's not a fruit tree. It grows avocados."

"You really are a genius, Albert. And you have me to thank for all the avocados it produces when you're schnorring off Doris."

"He's not a schnorrer," Doris said.

Albert frowned. "What does that mean?"

"Will you join us for dinner?" Doris said. "I can probably make something vegan."

"I can't. I'm working tonight."

Doris stepped over to him. "Thanks for taking care of the yard."

Slater rose and leaned in to kiss her cheek. "Love you."

Finally they went back inside. It would be so satisfying to punch Albert in the face, even just to bloody his nose. But he knew he'd never get away with it.

Pushing it out of his mind, he dropped to his knees and focused on the avocado—the feeling of the dark fertilizer in his hands as he massaged it into the soil around the base of the tree, the sound of the trowel biting into the ground, the rich smell of the earth. Eventually he was satisfied he'd churned the fertilizer in deep enough without nicking any of the roots.

Rising, he got the hose and soaked the ground around the tree for a few minutes, and inspected the dormant rosebushes and the lush bougainvillea. That hedge would need trimming in a week or so. After he put everything away, he went back through the side gate to his car.

Twilight was deepening, and as he backed into the street he flicked on his headlights. As he was approaching the freeway ramp, his phone rang—Conrad.

"What have you got for me?" Slater said, picking up.

"First, you have to thank me. You never do that."

"Why would I? I don't know yet whether there's anything to thank you for."

"It doesn't matter," Conrad said. "I did the work. Just say it."

"You know, it's like those homeless people who wipe your windshield at stoplights. They can't really demand full payment until they perform the labor."

"You're a piece of work, Slater, you know that?"

"Thank you," Slater said flatly, eyeing his side mirror as he accelerated onto the 110.

Conrad scoffed. "Two of the photos, the younger man and the woman, are civilians. Nothing more serious than a citation for speeding. She's got the lead foot, and he's got some parking violations. I'll send you their names."

That was the couple hooking up in the stall. It made sense that they weren't lowlifes—they were probably married to other people, and had fallen victim to Dawn's blackmail scheme.

"What about the other photo?"

"That older guy is bad news."

"What does that mean, exactly?" Slater said.

"He's known to the police. Works as a button man for the Eastern syndicate. His name is Baglio."

"Is there an address for him?"

"Not a current one, but his file lists one of his local associates. A guy named Ray. He works at a place called Beth Gellert. It's an Irish bar on Alvarado, right in your neighborhood."

"I know that place—you and I have been by

there. With the neon shamrock. It's not really an Irish bar. It's kind of a trendy joint, where the hep cats go to groove."

"So you'll fit right in," Conrad said.

"Whenever I get tangled up with that kind of crowd, they assume I'm either the bar-back or the bouncer."

Slater braked in the stop-and-go traffic. The lanes from the 101 joined the freeway here, and he focused on merging right through all the vehicles merging left, so that he could exit into his neighborhood.

"I can't imagine a guy like Baglio would be hanging out at a place like that. You've seen him—he's no kid."

"But that's the intel on him: Ray at Beth Gellert."

"That's what I got."

"This is useful information," Slater said.

"I'm thinking that's as close as I'm going to get to a thank-you."

"Well, considering your breathtaking simple-mindedness, I am a little surprised you were able to find all this in such a short time. But I guess that's about whoever you asked to help you."

Conrad sighed audibly. "You're welcome, Slater."

As he ended the call, he drove toward Alvarado. That bar was just a few blocks up. It was barely dark when he pulled up at the facade with the shamrock, lit up and glowing bright green, but there was already a short line on the sidewalk, a string of twenty-somethings waiting to get inside. Some of the women were in short skirts, and the men were in trendy suit jackets, like they were going clubbing. He was wrong about the name, he saw, wrong about this place—the black letters inside the shamrock said BRIDGET'S.

ELEVEN

S LATER PULLED BACK INTO the street and cruised to the end of the block, then pulled over to the curb. Looking at the map on his phone, the place Conrad had mentioned, Beth Gellert, was a different bar, two blocks farther up. He nosed into the traffic again and cruised past it.

The vibe of this place was more low-key, like a traditional Irish bar, with no neon and no lineup to get in, just a small painted sign and a dimly lit entrance. Slater backed into a meter spot in front and walked up to the door.

Inside there was a lot of dark wood, and high-backed booths along one wall. It wasn't busy at all—no one was sitting at the bar, and only one of the booths was occupied, by a couple of women drinking draft beer. Those two looked like regulars, glancing up at him as he stepped in, disinterest in their eyes. Behind the bar was a white-shirted bartender. The only other staffer was a bar-back, in the narrow space at the far end, unpacking bottles from a cardboard box.

Slater sat on a stool and waited for the bartender to approach. The guy had a square jaw, and a sullen expression, and his gray hair parted at the side, the way former military guys sometimes did. The chrome-plated name tag he was wearing on his shirt saved Slater some work—it revealed that this was Ray.

"What can I get for you?" Ray said. His dialect actually sounded Irish.

"A small of something light. A lager, if you have one on tap."

"That, I can do," he said, and stepped away, returning a minute later with a glass brimming with the golden liquid.

Slater set a twenty on the bar top. "Are you really from Ireland, or just practicing accents between acting gigs?"

Ray frowned. "I was born and raised in County Donegal."

"You could probably get acting work if you wanted. You have the right kind of face."

"Aren't you the charmer." Ray plucked the twenty and stepped over to the till.

Slater sipped his beer and watched him work. When he came back with his change, he spoke again.

"I'm looking for a guy named Baglio. Do you think he'll be in tonight?"

"I don't know that name," Ray said.

"Of course you don't, but if you did, I'd like to talk to him. I might have some work."

"I just told you I don't know him."

"I understand that," Slater said. "It's nothing heavy. I just need someone with some common sense to come with me to a business meeting."

"To hold your purse for you."

Slater lifted his glass and tipped it toward him. "You get the idea, Ray. You're smarter than you look."

"Who told you about this mythical Mr. Baglio? And why would you think I know anything about him?"

"A guy I know does some business with the city. He said Baglio knows what he's doing, and that he might work freelance sometimes."

Ray spread his palms on the bar. "Who was this person?"

"I'm not the kind of guy to kiss and tell, Ray. His business isn't any of my business. You know how it is."

"And what's your name, son?"

"John Slade," Slater said.

Ray frowned. "John, or Juan?"

"You know that most of the people in this neighborhood look more like me than like you, right?"

"I'm keenly aware of that."

"I've never been to Ireland," Slater said. "Are they all as racist as you?"

Ray raised his voice. "You keep your filthy tongue off Ireland."

Then his eyes flicked toward the entrance,

and his expression shifted. Slater heard the door swing closed. Looking over his shoulder, he recognized the face, the frame—it was Baglio walking in, dressed casually tonight, in a gray sweater and black jeans.

"There's the man," Slater said, and waved him over.

Baglio's eyes narrowed as he approached the bar, and from the corner of his eye, Slater saw Ray subtly shake his head. Baglio stepped up to them anyway.

"I was hoping I'd run into you tonight," Slater said.

"Do I know you?" Baglio said.

"Not yet, but have a seat—I'm buying."

"He says his name is John," Ray said. "I'm not sure if that's true."

Slater frowned. "You could have just carded me if you needed proof, officer."

"Who am I to turn down a free drink?" Baglio said.

Slater watched as he climbed onto the adjacent stool. His dialect sounded East Coast—New York or Philly. There wasn't room for a heater under that sweater, Slater decided. It made sense that he wasn't armed—you didn't carry unless you were on a job that required it.

Baglio nodded to Ray. "A pint of plain."

Ray scowled, and hesitated, then eyed Slater. "I've got my eye on you."

"I bet nobody messes with Ray," Slater said, watching him step away.

"They try to often enough." Baglio swiveled on his stool and looked Slater over. "So why are you looking for me, John?"

"It's work-related."

"I figured."

Ray stepped up and set down a pint of black beer with a thick brown head.

"That's what you call plain?" Slater said.

Ignoring him, Ray plucked a bill from his pile of change and stepped away.

"Cheers," Baglio said, and tapped his glass against Slater's, and took a gulp. "Now that I've got my drink, you've got about half a minute to tell me what it is that you want."

"That's not a lot of time. You must drink fast."

"I know you're not a civilian," Baglio said, eyeing him sidelong. "Who are you working for?"

Slater sipped his beer before he replied. "You had a meeting with a guy named Morales. He's on the city council. I'd like to talk about that."

Baglio chuckled. "You don't look like a cop."

"I'm not. But I have photos of the meet-up, and I could easily forward them to the cops, if you decide to stonewall me."

"I know that's not true. But full points for the bluff." He tipped his glass and took a drink.

Slater pulled out his phone and found one of the photos of him with Morales, a wad of cash in his hand. He held up the screen for Baglio to see, and swiped to the next image.

"Christ—where did you get those?" He frowned as Slater tucked his phone away, then clicked his tongue. "You know, I'm not too worried if the cops see that. They don't usually go after the messenger."

"They might not charge you," Slater said, "but they'll have a whole lot of awkward questions."

"What's your stake in this?"

"Someone is using those photos to extort Morales. I want to know the rest of the story."

"The photos tell you the part that matters. I delivered some cash to the councilmember in the men's room at the Baltimore Hotel."

"A fuck-ton of cash, I'd say."

"Three hundred grand."

"What was the money for, and who was it from?"

"It was nice to meet you, John. Thanks for the drink." Baglio took a gulp, and then slid off the barstool, and nodded to Ray.

"I'll walk you out," Slater said, and got up.

Baglio paused and looked him over, a wry smile on his face. "I know you're not packing, so I know you're not going to try to rough me up in the parking lot."

"You have dark thoughts, Baglio."

He gestured for Slater to go first, then followed him out onto the dark sidewalk. When Slater turned to face him, Baglio's eyes were hard.

"Time for you to shove off now. You're a punk, and you're wasting my time."

Stepping closer, Slater slapped him, right and then left, a rapid kovac. Baglio swatted his arm away, his eyes narrowing.

"Why would you do that to me when you know I can defend myself?"

The guy wasn't really upset about getting slapped, Slater realized. That calm demeanor was ominous—it meant his payback might be dire.

"I'm not a punk."

"But you're soft," Baglio said, and drew his arm back.

Slater saw it coming, and moved fast, and ducked the blow. He body-slammed Baglio into the stucco facade, one hand pinning his wrist, the other on his throat. With his free hand, Baglio grabbed a fistful of Slater's hair and pulled on it. Resisting the force, Slater lunged at him, smashing his forehead into Baglio's. His head snapped back into the stucco, and Slater tightened his grip on his throat, pressing hard into his body.

Baglio groaned and squeezed his eyes shut. His hand dropped out of Slater's hair. He took a few rapid breaths before he spoke.

"I just came out to see a friend and have a drink in peace. I don't need this bullshit."

"All you have to do is sing, brother," Slater said, "and the pain stops."

"You, my friend, have no idea what pain you're in for." He met Slater's eye. "Hold on. You've got a stiffy."

Slater hesitated. "It must be my car keys."

"What the hell kind of car do you drive? My keys don't swell up when I'm abusing someone."

There was something familiar in his gaze—not fear, but amusement, maybe, and excitement, and anticipation. Like whatever was going to happen next would feel really good or hurt a lot. Slater leaned in, close enough to smell his skin, redolent of sweat and soap. Baglio didn't recoil, and didn't try to pull his wrist out of Slater's grip, even though he knew he easily could. Slater extended his tongue and slowly licked his cheek.

Turning toward him, Baglio met his mouth. It tasted of bitter dark beer. The guy was good at this—intent, intuitive, eager, unlike his weary reaction to the scuffle.

After a moment Slater pulled away, and took a step back, and showed his palms. "No violence."

"You're the one who brought the Chicago how-do, remember?" Baglio rubbed his throat, his eyes flicking over Slater's form. "And the wood. You're a lot of man, John."

The front door of the bar swung open, and Ray stepped outside, holding a baseball bat on his shoulder.

"I noticed on the security camera that you were still being bothered by this gadfly," he said. "Do you need assistance, friend?"

Baglio waved a hand. "It's fine. We're just talking."

"It didn't look like that to me. Did he bite your ear?"

"Go back inside, Ray," Baglio said. "I can handle this."

Ray looked at Slater, raw hatred in his eyes, then back to Baglio, then turned on his heel and stepped through the door.

"You're probably married, huh," Baglio said.

"Why would you say that?"

"I never meet guys in this business who are available."

"I'm not available, if you want to take a yoga class together, or hike in Griffith Park, or shop for drapes, but I'll fuck you, if that's what you want."

"Is this some kind of scam?" Baglio said. "Who are you working for?"

"I told you that already. Morales. Listen, I live close to here—a couple minutes' drive." He gestured to the Thunderbird. "That's my ride."

Baglio eyed the vehicle, then looked at Slater. "So let's go."

Slater walked around the car and got behind the wheel, then reached over to unlock the passenger door.

"Is this a '77, or a '78?" Baglio said as he climbed in.

"You know your stuff. It's a '78."

"I think my pop had one of these. It was kind of a purple-maroon color. That thing went like a bat out of hell."

As Slater pulled away from the curb, he could feel Baglio's eyes on him.

"I usually trust my gut with people," Baglio said. "This feels just slightly off. Are you for real? You're not taking me for a ride, are you?"

"I'm not that guy. I will, however, let you ride my dick."

Baglio guffawed at that, and soon Slater turned into his alley, and nosed into his garage, and led the way upstairs to his apartment.

"Spartan," Baglio said, stepping inside and

looking around. "But functional."

"It works for what I need."

Slater bolted the door, and stood close to him. He reached for his face to caress his cheek. Before he could, Baglio grabbed his wrist, and pulled it away, and held firm.

"You want to play rough?" Slater said. "We can do that."

"Just checking."

"For what?"

Baglio chuckled, and let go of him, then put his hands on Slater's belt, pulling him closer. He kissed him, then moved to his neck, and his jaw. It felt like Baglio's mouth was all over him, everywhere at once. Pulling him closer, Slater could feel his woody.

"You're so fucking hot," Baglio mumbled.

"Take off your sweater."

Underneath he was wearing a white T-shirt, revealing a chest that was halfway muscular, halfway soft. Slater slid his hands under the fabric, shoving it up, and massaged his pecs. They were covered with downy hair.

Unbuttoning his own shirt, Slater led him to his bedroom. Baglio had his T-shirt off, and reached for Slater's belt, unbuckling it. Holding his gaze, he pulled Slater's fly open and popped the buttons. Something about the look in his eye, maybe just the eye contact itself, was a turn-on.

Pushing Slater's jeans down, Baglio dropped to one knee, and took him into his mouth, deftly working him for a minute, but not taking it too far. When he rose, Slater met his warm mouth, and reached for his fly to unzip his jeans. In a moment they were both naked.

Following him onto the futon, Baglio straddled him, lowering just enough of his weight onto Slater that he could feel the pressure, feel the heat of his skin, his wood pressing into him. Then he rolled onto his side, and Slater squeezed Baglio's cock. As he massaged it, Baglio spent a minute exploring Slater's body with his hands.

"You said you were going to fuck me," he said.

Slater rolled to the bedside table and grabbed a condom, then met his mouth as he rolled it on.

"Lie back," Baglio said, pushing him down.

Baglio grabbed the lube, and straddled his hips, and eased onto him. With his hands on his shoulders, then his arms, and his chest, Slater strained into him, panting with the intensity of it. Baglio was soon rocking back and forth. He was still hard, and Slater grabbed his cock and stroked him as they moved together. Baglio met his gaze again, with that look in his eye—part desire, part challenge—and Slater came, straining into him. In Slater's hand Baglio climaxed too.

Panting, Baglio flopped onto his back. "That was so fucking hot. Do you have any idea how hot that was?"

Slater covered his eyes with his arm and grunted in acknowledgment. A few minutes later, Baglio rose, and Slater heard the water running in the bathroom. When he came back, he had a damp towel in hand, and gently wiped Slater's belly, and his junk, and then threw the towel on the floor. Slater grinned, watching him work. It was a sweet gesture.

Baglio stretched out and pulled him closer. Slater rolled onto his side, letting himself be cradled in his big arms. He drifted off and was only vaguely aware of Baglio sitting up, and then the familiar tinkling sound of his own belt buckle.

"Slater Ibáñez," Baglio said, Anglicizing his surname as *ee*-buh-*nez*. "I knew you didn't look like a John."

Waking, Slater saw that he'd taken his wallet out of his jeans, and was studying his driver's license.

He sat up, and grabbed the wallet, and tossed it on the floor. "Snoop."

Baglio chuckled and stretched out beside him, running a hand on Slater's chest, and his neck, and fingering his Adam's apple.

"You totally let me hit you tonight," Slater said. "I know you could have stopped me."

"The paintbrush doesn't really qualify as fisticuffs, though, does it? It's more about focusing someone's attention."

"That's exactly what it's about. Although on the West Coast it's called a kovac."

"I knew what you were trying to do."

"But you didn't lose your cool," Slater said. "You just let me do it. It made me think I was in for a serious beatdown."

"I guess I wanted you to hit me. I'm not sure why." He took a breath and caressed Slater's chest. "Something about getting hurt by a pretty boy. It's a familiar pattern. I was acting it out again."

"It sounds like you've had your head shrunk."

"Just once," Baglio said. "For a few months. It helped me a lot—I changed careers, and significantly reduced my stress level."

"Here or back east?"

"I was here already. I had to leave New York. That city was so rough. It felt like it was grinding me down. Then my shrink said, 'Maybe it's you. Maybe you're the one who's too rough. Did you ever think of that?' So I ventilated him."

Slater met his eye. "Seriously?"

"Of course not." Baglio chuckled. "I'm not crazy. Plus he had a point."

"Rewind a little here. You called me 'pretty.' That's just wrong."

Baglio caressed his cheek with a thick thumb. "But you are, sweet petal. Like the first daisies of spring in the meadow, trembling in the gentle breeze."

Slater had to laugh. "You may be rough, Baglio, but you know how to lay your mack down."

"Are you really working for Morales?"

"He's a friend of my mother's."

"Wow. I know you didn't just make that up."

"So who hired you to make the payoff?"

"I can't tell you that," Baglio said. He took Slater's hand and interlaced their fingers. "It would be unprofessional. But I can say that these payments are customary. They clear away the red tape and political opposition to land development projects."

"So you were repping a developer."

"I didn't say that. But it's a reasonable conclusion." He kissed the back of Slater's hand. "What I can't figure out is how you got those pictures."

"They were taken from waist level. That makes me think the camera was hidden in a handbag or a briefcase. It had to be whoever was there with you. Did Morales bring an assistant?"

"I'm not a tyro at this kind of work, Slater."

"So no one else was there."

"We were alone—I made sure of it. I did a sweep of the stalls."

"Curious," Slater said, and put his arm over his eyes.

He woke when Baglio was getting dressed.

"I have to go," he said.

"Let me give you my card."

Baglio eyed him as he buckled his belt. "So you want to hang out again."

"Why not?" Slater sat up, and grabbed his jeans, and dug out his business card.

"Insurance," Baglio said, studying it. "That's a great cover. You can poke into almost anything."

"It's legit, though. I do investigate insurance cases."

Baglio pulled his phone out of his jeans and tapped at the screen. "I just sent you my number. So you can't say you didn't call me because you didn't have it."

When he followed him to the front door, Baglio turned to kiss him. He was so good at it, so responsive, and Slater got lost in it. Eventually he pulled back.

"Get out of here," Slater said, "or I'll have to pound you again."

Baglio grinned at that as he left. Once Slater had flipped the deadbolt, he went to the kitchen cupboard to pull out a fifth. He poured his ration of the amber liquid, and slammed it, then took a pull from the bottle.

It felt like it was late, and he was tired. Back in bed, he could feel the warmth in his belly, gradually spreading, slowing things down. He didn't usually volunteer for repeats with his hookups—it felt sappy, and needy, and weak. But Baglio knew stuff, and he just might reveal more.

TWELVE

LYING IN BED, GRADUALLY waking up to the light streaming in from outside, Slater thought about Baglio. He'd said that no one else was there when he'd paid Morales, and he'd framed that as a standard business practice. It made sense that you wouldn't have observers hanging around when you were delivering that much cash. Every pair of eyeballs exponentially multiplied the potential problems.

From his bedside table he grabbed his phone, then swiped through the photos he'd scanned of Baglio with Morales. Each image had exactly the same framing, the same view of the urinals and the out-of-focus sink. He'd been wrong about a third player, wrong about someone hiding it in a hand-bag—the camera was fixed, like the one above the restroom stall.

Climbing out of bed, he looked in the Frigidaire.

Of course there was nothing to eat. He took out the jar of olives and munched on a few, then swirled a scoop of brown powder into a mugful of water and microwaved it. After he slurped some down, he got dressed, pulling on a dark shirt and yesterday's jeans.

As he backed out of his garage, the light was hazy and diffuse this morning, but he put on his sunglasses anyway, pushing them up onto his head. Minutes later he was downtown, and pulled into the garage under the square, across the street from the Baltimore Hotel.

Slater knew where the restrooms were, back by the hotel's ballrooms, and he walked the wide corridor, glancing up at its ornate coffered ceiling, and pulled his sunglasses down over his eyes. The place was quiet, with no events in the grand rooms this early on Monday morning. No one was in the men's room when he went in. He sized up the layout, the row of urinals, and figured out where Baglio had made the handoff to Morales. It was a corner, far from the door, where they would have had time to react, time to conceal the dough if anyone else came in.

Standing at the sink, he ran the tap and looked sidelong from behind his dark glasses to study the wall where the photos must have been taken from. Nothing looked out of place, but then he noticed the motion-sensor box. It was white, the same color as the tile, and mounted at waist level on that wall. Usually those were overhead, high up, where it was harder to tamper with them.

Peering at it from his vantage at the sink, he saw there was a dark spot below the frosted bubble for the sensor. That easily could be a lens. He turned off the tap and walked toward it, studying the device as he passed it. It had to be bogus—a stealthy camera, the kind of thing Svetlana built.

As he walked back into the empty corridor, he pushed his sunglasses up into his hair. That camera was concealed, but it hadn't been purpose-built for blackmail. If Dawn had planted it, she couldn't have known Morales would take a payoff right there. But it did have an excellent view of the urinals.

In his pants his phone buzzed, and he pulled it out to check. It was a text from Morales:

Updates?

Slater stopped in the broad hallway to thumb-type a reply:

Are you in your office?

His response came a moment later:

I'm here. Stop by.

Rather than move his car and pay for more overpriced parking, he left it under the square and walked the few blocks to city hall. In the foyer he stopped at the security desk.

"I have an appointment with Bud Morales," Slater said, even though the guard hadn't looked up at him yet. "Are you going to hinder me, or can I go up?"

"What's your name?"

"Ibáñez," he said flatly.

The guy typed on the computer and peered at the screen. "You're on the list," he said finally. "Go ahead."

Slater scoffed and went to the elevators.

There was no sign of Morales in the hallway this time, and he went to the big double doors that bore an oversize gold plaque engraved with Morales's name. This was the front office, with lots of dark wood inside, and in a corner stood another city flag, draped carefully around its stand.

On the desk was a man in his twenties, with dark Latin hair, wearing a chocolate-brown suit, a shade similar to the ones his boss wore.

"Where's Morales?" Slater said, walking toward him.

The guy's eyes flicked over him. "Do you have an appointment?"

"He called me," Slater said, raising his voice. "And now I'm here. Stop wasting my fucking time."

"I'm the councilmember's personal assistant. Perhaps you could explain your issue."

Moving closer, Slater rested his palms on the desk and leaned toward him.

"Is that what they're calling sycophants nowadays?" Slater demanded. "Does the 'personal' mean you're fucking him?"

The guy scowled. "Of course not. Why would you say that?"

"You wouldn't be the first twinkie to go down on his boss. Sometimes you have to give a little head to get ahead, so to speak."

The guy inched backward in his chair. "What exactly do you need from the councilmember?"

"Get Morales out here, or I'm going to find him myself."

He hesitated, so Slater reached for a stack of manila folders sitting in a tray at the side of his desk, and holding his gaze, pushed it off the edge. The tray hit the carpet with a thud, and the paper splayed around it.

"You asshole," the guy shouted.

"Watch your tongue, or I'll rip it out and shove it down your throat."

The door beside his desk opened, and Morales stepped in, wearing his slick brown suit. His brow furrowed as he looked at Slater, then his assistant.

"Come in," he said finally.

"Who is this psycho?" the guy demanded.

"Settle down, now," Morales said to him, and waved Slater in.

Morales led him through a conference room, where two women sat at the big table, under the high windows, working on laptops. Neither of them looked up as he and Morales walked through. The next room was the office Slater had been in before.

"Have a seat." Morales closed the door behind him and then dropped into his chair.

"I can't stay long."

He gestured broadly. "How are things going?"

"I'm learning more about Dawn and the scam she's running."

"Like what?"

"She has a rap sheet, and she's currently on

parole. Maybe you knew that already."

"I didn't."

Slater nodded. "Also, you're not the only one she has on the hook. I've found a handful of others."

"So it's a full-time business. Is it all sex stuff?"

"What I've seen definitely is."

"Am I going to have to pay her?"

"Give me a little time to dig deeper. I think I may have found a way to shut her down."

Morales laughed, his tone deep. "That would be the optimal outcome."

"Not just for you—for all her victims." Slater frowned. "So in the photos that Dawn has, who was the woman you were with?"

"Did Dawn show them to you?" Morales gazed at him intently.

"She didn't show me anything."

"I'm not going to tell you about her."

"OK, so what exactly was in those photos?" Slater demanded.

"I already told you that. I only saw a small sample. A snippet."

"If you showed me what she sent you, it might give me a lead. Maybe I could figure out who the photographer was."

Morales shook his head. "It seems to me you're doing just fine without seeing that trash."

"All right. If that's how you want to play it." Slater put his hands on his hips. "Have you heard from Dawn lately?"

"Not since I brought you on board."

"If she reaches out, I told her you're having trouble raising the funds, so stick to that. Tell her she needs to go through me. Definitely don't give her any cash. I think she's broke, and I want to keep it that way."

"Stalling her is only going to work for so long."

"Don't worry about that," Slater said. "Not having funds will make her more desperate. Even so, she's not going to publish anytime soon."

"How do you know that?"

"She's working other angles with other players. Those need time to play out. Plus if she publishes, she knows she'll get nothing."

"With the same photos? What other angles?"

"I only saw a snippet," Slater said flatly.

Morales frowned. "You're working for me. Don't lose sight of that."

Slater gestured to the side door. "Can I go out that way? Your assistant makes me uncomfortable."

"Be my guest." Morales rose as Slater walked out, and called after him, "Keep me informed."

Morales had been lying to him from the beginning, Slater thought, walking back to the elevators. Lying about all of it. That alone wasn't surprising—everybody lied, all the time, about everything—but it made it more complicated, gave him more parts to juggle. And it meant that even though he'd taken the guy's money, he felt no compulsion to tell him everything.

Out in the wan winter light on Main Street, he saw that there was a text from Andy:

News.

Walking south, Slater headed over to Broadway, and into Andy's building. When he answered the door, Andy was wearing his usual boxers and a T-shirt, and greeted Slater with that smile.

"So what have you got for me?" Slater said, following him in.

Andy went to his desk chair and sat down, swiveling toward him. "Somehow your target has … been able to use her alias as if it were a legal name. That's how she … avoided detection as a felon in some of this stuff."

"What kind of stuff?"

"You can sit, if you want."

Slater grabbed one of the chairs at his little table and sat on it backward, facing him, and folded his arms on the back.

"Dawn Snowden drew public benefits for … a while. That's not supposed to be possible if … you're a convicted felon. But then Dawn … Strezlecki was the name with the felony conviction."

"Good to know."

"Her alias is also the owner of … a dozen or so very busy internet domains," Andy said. "There are a bunch of … different names and skins on the sites, but they all … lead to two root properties, one called … Public Weenie, and the other is Public Cooch."

"It's porn?"

"Exactly. A porn site of candid shots … of guys at urinals and women in … restroom stalls."

"I guess there's a market for everything," Slater said.

"I looked at the front page and the … teasers. It's stomach-churning stuff."

Slater pursed his lips and stared out the big multipane windows, thinking it through.

"Is that helpful?" Andy said finally.

"Very. It fits with what I've uncovered."

"You knew she was a porn boss?"

"I didn't, but I think I inadvertently found one of her source cameras." Slater got up. "What do I owe you?"

"Let's call it five hundred."

"Christ, toots, is that the only number you know?"

"Is the information worth it to you?" Andy demanded.

"It is," he said, counting the C-notes from his wad. "But there are lots of other numbers. Smaller ones."

Andy took the bills and tossed them on his desk. "Do you have time to mess around?"

"I wish I could, but I have to act on this." Slater leaned in and briefly kissed him. "Bye, beautiful."

Once he was downstairs, and out on Broadway, Slater phoned Baglio.

"So you can't get enough of me," Baglio said when he picked up.

"I had fun last night. Do you have a minute to meet up?"

"For you, I've got all day. What's up?"

"I learned some more about those photos," Slater said. "Where are you?"

"Downtown, at that bookstore on Eighth."

Slater suppressed his first reaction—*What's a guy like you doing in a bookstore?* Instead, he said, "Meet me at that diner on Seventh. It's right around the corner. I'll buy you breakfast."

It was just a few blocks, and Slater decided to walk, down through the Jewelry District. When he stepped inside the diner, Baglio was at the counter, parked on a stool, wearing a blue nylon jacket and chinos. He'd picked the side with a view of the entrance and the front window. The guy had good instincts—it was exactly the spot Slater would have chosen.

"Did you order?" Slater said, climbing onto the stool beside him.

"I did." Baglio squeezed his shoulder with his big meaty hand.

The waitress, a slight woman with pale blue eyes and freckles, stepped up and raised her eyebrows. "What'll it be, hon?"

"Java, and a bowl of oatmeal with soy milk, on the same check."

She nodded and stepped away.

"So what did you find out about your photos?" Baglio said.

"I'm pretty sure there's a hidden camera in that men's room."

"That would explain how they took them without me noticing. I thought I was losing my touch. Who's the trash bag who did that? I'll punch his lights out."

"It's a her," Slater said.

"She put a camera next to the urinals? What's

her endgame?"

"Urinal porn."

"That's a thing?"

Slater shrugged. "It seems so."

"She sounds like a real bearcat."

"There's an accomplice who runs the websites. I took a run at him already."

The food arrived, and Slater ate his oatmeal while Baglio dug into a club sandwich. When he finished, he wiped his hands vigorously on a napkin, then balled it up and dropped it on the plate.

"I can still smell you on my skin," Baglio said quietly.

Slater eyed him. "I liked being all over your skin."

He chuckled, and looked away, his face reddening. It was surprising that a guy like Baglio would blush at anything.

"Want to do a nooner?" Slater said.

Baglio put a hand on his neck. "I can't believe you're real."

Leaning in, Slater kissed him. His mouth tasted of coffee. Why was this guy so compelling? The way his tongue moved, and his lips, it was all kind of perfect. He could feel his dick tightening in his jeans.

"Get a room, fellas," a woman's voice said.

Slater pulled away. It was the pale waitress, standing there with her hands on her hips, scowling at them.

"Are you kidding me?" Slater demanded, glaring at her.

She laughed. "I'm just messing with you. Man, the look on your face." She set the check on the counter between them. "Sorry I interrupted—I don't actually care whether you mess up his makeup."

Watching her step away, Baglio said, "She thinks I wear makeup? I must have amazing skin."

"You do have amazing skin." Slater peeled some bills off his wad and set them on the counter with the check, then followed Baglio out to the street.

"Where's your flivver?" Baglio said.

"In the garage under Pershing Square."

"Can we go to your place? I'm kind of staying with people. It would be awkward."

Slater briefly squeezed him around the shoulders, and they walked toward the square.

THIRTEEN

U P IN SLATER'S APARTMENT, he locked lips with Baglio again, and ran his hands into his short hair, damp now with sweat, maybe from the effort of climbing two flights of stairs.

"Can I do you?" Baglio said, pulling back.

"You mean fuck me? Sure, if that's what you want."

Slater led him to the bedroom, and they both got undressed. Sitting on the edge of the futon, Slater pulled him onto it, and explored his body with his hands. He must have had muscle tone once, and even though he was softer now, his body was still a turn-on.

Squeezing his cock and exploring his mouth, Baglio was soon hard, and Slater grabbed a condom and rolled it on him, then handed him the lube.

"I've got a bit of performance anxiety," Baglio said quietly.

"It doesn't matter what we do. I have no expectations."

"I want to fuck you. It's just that you're so beautiful."

Slater stifled a scoff. "You're not seeing the whole picture."

"I can see you, and touch you." He ran his hand across Slater's chest.

"That's only the surface. I'm trouble, son."

Baglio snorted. "I'm old enough to be your pop."

Slater squeezed his cock, eliciting a gasp. "Don't think about that. What do you want to do to me?"

"I want to fuck you," he said softly.

"Excuse me?" Slater demanded.

"I want to fuck you," he said, louder this time.

Slater slapped his face. "So bring it on."

Baglio reflexively grabbed his wrist, then tossed it away, and glared at him, his surprise shifting to anger. He pushed up Slater's knee, and worked a thumb into him, a half snarl on his face.

He was in work mode now, Slater saw—and he had no performance anxiety about that. Slater laced his fingers behind his head and jutted his chin, a challenge in his eyes, his lip curling in a sneer, affecting the angry hoodlum.

"Oh, you are in for it," Baglio growled.

He shifted closer, and eased into him, his hands gripping Slater's thighs. His face contorted, and panting with the intensity of it, he started to thrust. Slater winced and ran a hand into his hair. Soon Baglio was pounding him, and then he made one last thrust as he came, and whimpered, and collapsed beside him.

Mouthing his jaw and his neck, Baglio grabbed Slater's cock and worked it. With his nose in Baglio's ear, smelling his hair, Slater soon climaxed, with a spasm that racked his body.

Baglio rolled onto his back and slid a thick arm under Slater's neck. Once his breathing had slowed, Slater traced the ragged double scar that ran from his collarbone almost to his nipple.

"It looks like you had a brawl with a werewolf."

"Things got a little out of hand that day. I was still figuring out how to do my job. It was a long time ago." He put his palm on top of Slater's hand and squeezed it. "So why do you live in this place?"

"It has a private garage."

"I guess that's a plus."

"I know it's a dump. It's where I need to be."

"I'm not judging your apartment. In New York this would be a million-dollar condo."

"How long have you been out here?" Slater said.

"It must be pushing five years by now."

"Why don't you have your own place?"

"I don't make a lot of money anymore. I quit working for the syndicate, so I'm doing odd jobs, living off savings. It's cheaper to stay with friends." He met Slater's eye. "Don't get the wrong idea—it's not like I'm on the skids. I'm staying in a decent place. One of those garden-shed conversions. There's lots of trees."

"How do you get gigs these days?"

"From my old contacts in the business, and

word of mouth. Ray is a good source. He meets lots of people."

"He told me he'd never heard of you."

"That's because no one introduced you to him," Baglio said. "He didn't know who you were."

"He was ready to knock my block off last night with that baseball bat," Slater said. "So why did you quit the syndicate?"

"It's all or nothing with them. You do what you're told or it's the dirt nap."

"How did you get out?"

"I paid my way. Everything has a price in that world."

"How did you meet the person who hired you to pay off Morales?"

Baglio chuckled. "I knew you'd come around to that." He lifted his forearm to give Slater's neck a playful squeeze before he continued. "The guy who hired me works for developers. His name is Goh." Baglio spelled it. "I think he's Korean, and I know he works for the Chinese companies that are building all those empty condo towers around the stadium."

Goh—that was the name Dawn had used. The guy she'd met at the hotel bar.

"I don't know anything else about him," Baglio said.

"Thanks for breaking your confidentiality code."

"All that does is save you some time. Goh is a lowlife. You would have run across him eventually."

Slater put his arm over his eyes, relishing the warmth of Baglio's skin as he dozed. After a while he could feel Baglio's breath on his elbow, and he

178

moved his arm again to look. Baglio was watching him. He had that look in his eye—emotional longing.

"What's going on?" Slater said.

"I'm just sad. I really like you, but I know you're only sleeping with me to pump me for information."

"I'm sleeping with you because you're hot."

"Bullshit. I know I'm not."

"I disagree," Slater said flatly. "And if I only needed information, I would have beaten it out of you."

Baglio chuckled. "In your dreams. I could clean your clock any day of the week."

"Yeah, I know you could." Slater watched him for a moment. "You're desirable, brother. Don't let anyone tell you otherwise."

"Why don't you have a boyfriend?"

"I don't really do that."

Baglio caressed his belly. "It probably wouldn't work anyway. I'm kind of a mess."

"You seem functional to me."

"I'm East Coast messed up, not Cali messed up."

Slater chuckled. "It's different?"

"LA messed up is sloppier, maybe. At first I liked the lack of structure in the business out here. There's less hierarchy. It felt like the Wild West."

"I can't compare," Slater said. "I've never lived anywhere else."

"It's not like it matters. I'm finding that I'm the same person no matter where I go."

"That sounds familiar—I bet your shrink mentioned that."

"You're right. It had the ring of truth. Amazing how a few words can make you see the world from a whole different perspective. Anyway, I like it here, but California hasn't fixed me."

Baglio got up and went into the bathroom. A minute later he came back with a towel and threw it to Slater, then stepped into his underpants.

"I had fun," Slater said, watching him get dressed.

"I need to go."

"Don't hustle on my account. I'm in no rush."

"I don't want to fall for you," Baglio said, eyeing him sidelong, "and that means I can't be around you."

Slater didn't know what to say to that. He could feel his heart pounding. Once he had his shoes on, Baglio mumbled a farewell and walked out. Slater heard the front door close, and lay there for a while, thinking about Baglio. Why was it so hard for people to keep their emotional stuff separate from the sex?

Picking up his phone, he searched for "Goh" and "developer," and quickly found a flashy website. It claimed that Goh was a real estate agent, with a portrait of him standing in front of a spiffy office building that towered above him. His arms were folded, and a big smile was plastered on his face. The text explained that he specialized in commercial properties.

Farther down the search results was an article on a news website, dated a few months back, titled "Following the Money in LA's Growth." Scrolling through it, the journalist claimed that the city's planning rules were routinely bent and broken to improve things for developers. She mentioned Goh by name as the broker of a series of deals that got huge city tax breaks in exchange for including low-income housing. The bait-and-switch came later in the process, when the developers somehow got exemptions to leave out the low-income housing without the city revisiting the tax assessment.

Slater gritted his teeth, annoyed at the blatant corruption, the unfairness of it. It was all part of the same problem—luxury building projects that paid no taxes, crooked officials like Morales taking payoffs, and sixty thousand people sleeping rough on the city's streets. This is why he tried not to pay attention to the news.

The journalist's byline at the top of the article cited her name as Nell Pilapil, and when he clicked on her thumbnail portrait, he was surprised to find her profile included an email address and a phone number. He dialed and got her voice mail.

"I'm an insurance investigator," Slater told the machine. "I read your article about a real estate operative named Goh. I want to talk to you about this guy."

Finally climbing out of bed, Slater washed up, then looked in the pantry cupboard for food, finding nothing but dust and the bourbon. The pair of amber bottles sat there silent, beautiful in their stoic patience, waiting for him to crack the cap. But not yet.

On the shelf below there actually was something

to eat, a little packet of saltines from a forgotten takeout order. He was munching on them when his phone rang, with a number he didn't know, in the 213 area code. Picking up, he answered, "Ibáñez."

"My name is Pilapil," a woman's voice said. "I'm returning your call. What's your interest in Mr. Goh?"

"I've been investigating him in relation to a case I'm working on," Slater said, stepping over to the window that looked over the street. Twilight was already setting in, the streetlights illuminated. "I might have found some dirt, and I thought you might be able to verify it or debunk it."

"It sounds like we should talk," she said.

"I can meet you now if you've got time."

"My beat is the Civic Center. I'm still down here." She named a coffeehouse. "Can you meet me there?"

"Is that the place by police headquarters? Will it still be open at this hour?"

"It's open," she said. "I'm sitting here now."

Slater ended the call and went into his bedroom to pull on his jeans and grab a clean shirt, then trotted down the stairs to his garage and drove downtown. It took a minute to find a meter spot, as there weren't any right near the coffeehouse.

Walking back toward the place, in the fading light he saw that there were live oaks planted along the sidewalk on the other side of the street, and magnolias lining this side. The city must just put in whatever saplings they found for cheap. Either that or they'd hired a schizophrenic to do the planning.

There were a few people sitting around the coffeehouse, even though it was after caffeine hours. Most of them were alone and staring at laptops, their sullen features illuminated by the blue glow of their screens. A woman waved at him when he stepped in.

Nell was slight and had her dark hair pulled back. She was wearing a black sweater and red-rimmed eyeglasses, with a little espresso cup in front of her.

Approaching the table, Slater greeted her.

"Do you want to grab a coffee?" she said.

He went to the counter and ordered a soy latte, then once he had the cup in hand, sat across from her.

"You waved at me the second I came in," Slater said. "How did you know it was me?"

"Your name matches your skin tone, for one, and the way you're dressed fits your occupation."

"You're sharp," he said, and sipped his coffee. He'd done the same thing with her, of course—her name was Tagalog, and it fit her looks. He'd identified her the moment he'd stepped in.

"It's my job. Do you have a business card?"

Slater produced one from his hip pocket, and Nell studied it for a moment before she tucked it away.

"So what kind of insurance claim are you working, and what did you find out about Goh?"

"I can't really talk about the case," Slater said. "It doesn't concern Goh directly. Some ancillary information came up—I might have evidence of him making a substantial covert cash payment to a politician."

"What politician? What's the evidence?"

"I can't share it with you, at least not yet. But it's solid."

"Playing it coy." Nell sighed. "I guess that's OK."

"What can you tell me that wasn't in your article?"

"Articles, plural," she said. "There have been several. I only publish stuff I have documentation for, but if you read between the lines, you'll pick up that I suspect he's in bed with several city councilmembers. The ones on the planning and land use committee. They've pushed through extreme variances for several big projects that Goh was involved with."

"Goh made sure the developers got the tax breaks without the requirement for low-income housing."

"Exactly. Among other variances."

"Like what?" Slater said, wrapping his hands around his coffee cup.

"Well, one of those buildings is eighty feet taller than the zoning allows for. They're not supposed to put the parking at street level anymore, because it alienates pedestrians, but with all those buildings the garages are at ground level. If you've been on the 10 lately you've seen the totally illegal block-long video billboard that one of the councilmembers pushed through. But the worst thing is the low-income variances." Nell eyed him for a moment. "It sounds like you know how the game works. These assholes are putting up exclusively luxury apartments and condos, even though city regulations state there's a minimum low-income housing requirement. They're supposed to be helping solve the housing crisis. What they're really doing is making it worse. But the rules don't apply if you're working with Mr. Goh."

"It sounds like he's good at what he's doing."

"All this stuff is public knowledge," she said, waving a hand, "at least for anyone who's paying attention. So I know you don't owe me anything. But I'd really like to see the details on whatever you've uncovered."

"I'm thinking it's part of the same story: Goh paying off a politician." Slater sat up. "Once I've concluded my research, I might be able to pass something on to you."

"Exclusively," she said, holding his gaze.

Slater shrugged. "Why not? I don't know anyone else who cares about this."

Nell rubbed her forehead. "Unfortunately that's part of the problem. When journalism gets defunded, no one's left to watch the store. The rats get to run rampant."

"You're watching," Slater said, and met her eye. "I read what you wrote, and it made my blood boil."

———◆———

IT WAS DARK OUT as Slater walked back to his car, then drove to his office. No one was around the building, and when he got upstairs, the lights were off. He poked his head into Max's office to make sure it was empty, then eyed the statue of Rey

Pascual, and double-clicked his tongue in greeting.

At his desk he put his feet up and pulled the keyboard into his lap, then spent some time reading more about city council. As she'd told him, Nell had written several other articles, and there was a string of commentary pieces from citizen watchdog groups, although none of them had as much tangible evidence as Nell had uncovered. More recently the feds had started investigating sleaze at city hall—two councilmembers were already under felony indictment, and it looked like more of them, along with several city staffers, were in the crosshairs.

Why wasn't this bigger news, he wondered. Digging deeper, he found that some academic had done a study of local government corruption, and there were proportionally more instances of it here than anywhere else in the country except Chicago.

Historically there were stories of graft and sleaze dating back to the pueblo era. In the 1920s a wealthy stage mother had paid a corrupt DA for years and years not to charge her with murdering a film director. In the 1940s a newspaper baron pressured the sheriff into burying the hunt for a killer who later murdered the Black Dahlia.

Maybe all the current corruption wasn't all that newsworthy because it had always been part of the system, baked into the city's DNA. Still, it pissed him off that one of Doris's friends was at the heart of it today.

Slater checked the time and then locked his computer, tossing the keyboard onto the desktop. It was that time of day, time to find a hookup, either on an app or at a bar on the way to his apartment. There were at least three places between here and there—one with entitled white guys, one with Latin guys, and one that was kind of mixed black and white. But hitting on chumps in a bar was a lot of freaking work. Plus he'd been with Baglio today, not all that long ago. Maybe he could take a night off.

As he was getting up, his phone rang, and he checked the screen—it was Dawn. When he picked up, he said, "Ibáñez."

"Where's my money?" she demanded.

"I assume it's in the boss's office. He told me to swing by there tomorrow to pick it up and take it over to you."

"Payment is overdue. He's going to have to add a thousand."

"I'll let him know," Slater said. "But if you keep changing the terms, it might further delay things."

"No more delays, you goon," she shouted. "I'm the one in charge."

"I understand that. Did you talk to Morales today?"

"He said I should call you."

"That's right," Slater said. "He's a busy man, and he tasked me to deal with the trash."

"Fuck you," she shouted, "and bring me my money, or the pictures go live."

"I heard you the first time, Dawn," he said, and ended the call.

It sounded like she was getting stressed, he thought, riding the elevator down to the street.

Money must be tight. Despite the threat, she wasn't going to publish yet, as it wasn't just about waiting on Morales. She was also waiting on Goh—so all she had was bluster.

Driving out of downtown, he pulled into his garage and went upstairs to his apartment. In the cupboard he opened the almost empty fifth, leaving the full one beside it. Not bothering with a tumbler, he drained it, relishing the burn in his throat, the fumes in his nose. This didn't even count toward his ration, he decided, because it was just the dregs. Most of the alcohol had probably evaporated already anyway.

Cracking the seal on the new bottle, he poured his ration into a tumbler and went to sit in his recliner, watching the sky outside. The house music would be starting to get good at this hour, and he put on the radio.

Waking later, he found his glass empty, and went back to the kitchen. He should probably stop, but then again, it couldn't be all that late. He poured another half tumbler, and slurped at it, and coughed at the fumes. Back in his chair, he set the glass on the carpet and got comfortable. Why were the nights so damn long, and why was he always alone? The bourbon was the only thing that got him through it. He closed his eyes and listened to the radio. The bourbon, and maybe the music.

FOURTEEN

W AKING IN HIS OWN bed, Slater's head hurt as he sat up. It wasn't that bad, he decided, looking around. The room wasn't spinning. Rising, he went to the kitchen. There were no clean glasses, and the ones beside the sink bore the nauseating smell of booze. He drank water by cupping his hands under the kitchen faucet. Lucky for him, Rosa was supposed to come straighten up sometime this week.

After he washed up, he crawled back into bed and checked his phone.

"Damn it," he muttered, under his breath. He'd phoned Doris last night. Forty seconds. He must have spoken to her. Squeezing his eyes shut, he tried to recall the conversation, but he just couldn't retrieve it.

He took a breath and dialed Doris's number.

"What's wrong?" she said when she picked up.

"What do you mean, 'What's wrong'? Can't I phone you without it being a crisis?"

"You never phone me, period," Doris said. "Except when I'm asleep and you're liquored up."

"I called you last night."

"You say that like you're not sure."

"What did I say?" Slater said, rubbing his forehead.

"You said my friend Bud Morales is trash."

"That's all?"

"Why would you characterize him that way? What did you find out about him?"

"I'm close to some conclusions," Slater said, "but I'm not quite there yet."

"Did you have an argument with Bud?"

"Nothing like that."

She lowered her voice. "Did you see his sex photos?"

"I'll tell you what I know once I wrap things up."

"All right. Well, feel better."

"I don't need to feel better," he said flatly. "I'm fine."

"Drink tomato juice for the hangover."

Slater hesitated. "I apologize for waking you last night."

"You didn't wake me. You left a voice mail. My phone didn't ring—I took you off my do-not-disturb exception list."

"Why would you do that?" he demanded. "I'm your son."

"Because you call me in the middle of the night to tell me that my friends are trash."

"Oh, god," he muttered.

"You need to get the drinking under control, Slater."

"It is. I was just having a rough night."

"Albert knows a detox place in Malibu. He says it's very comfortable."

"That's never going to happen. And don't be gossiping with that man about my personal stuff. I'm hanging up now."

Setting his phone aside, he stared at the half-open closet for a while, the row of shirts on hangers. His head still hurt. Eventually he pushed himself out of bed, and got dressed, and drove to a diner in Koreatown.

He picked a table along the wall, away from the window. When the waitress approached him, he ordered rice and kimchi.

"Do you have tomato juice?" he said.

"Sure."

After he'd eaten, his head didn't hurt as much, and his mind felt sharper. Goh's office was around here, he remembered, and he looked it up on his phone. It was just a few blocks.

Out on the street, he fed the meter where he'd parked the Thunderbird, then walked toward Goh's office building.

The sprawling green lawn out front looked like a golf course. It was such a poor choice for this town, like something out of the last century. Inside, the lobby was lined with Korean screen art. No way was it antique—there was too much of it, dozens of panels. The images were of medieval characters surrounded by fields of gold paint.

There was a security desk, and the guard glanced up as he walked past, but he didn't say anything. Unless there was a high-stakes tenant like a bank or a government office, they didn't tend to bother people during business hours, as long as it looked like you knew where you were going.

Back by the elevators, the directory on the wall said Goh's office was on 28. That must be close to the top of this building. It meant that Goh had Western values about real estate—from what Slater had seen, Asian companies preferred to be a couple of floors above street level, not on the high floors.

When he got off the elevator, he found Goh's suite, and stepped inside. The front office was roomy but not pretentious, with the reception desk and some lounge chairs done in blond wood and pastel fabrics. No one was here, although he could hear the faint sound of a printer or a photocopier somewhere nearby. A couple of doors led off this room. Only one of them was closed. Walking over to it, he pushed it open and stepped inside.

It was a corner office that had tall windows on two sides, with a dramatic view of the hills, the eastern part of Hollywood, and the towers on Bunker Hill. A conference table sat at one end, and near the windows was a big desk. Behind it sat the guy who'd met Dawn at the hotel bar—Goh. His hair was slicked back, and his feet were on the desktop, ankles crossed. When Slater stepped in, he set his laptop aside, and sat up, scowling at him.

"Who are you?" he demanded. "How did you get past my assistant?"

"There's no one out there. I guess I got lucky."

"What do you want?"

"You and I have some mutual acquaintances, Mr. Goh," Slater said, stepping closer to his desk. "Including Dawn Snowden."

"I've never heard that name."

"I'm not surprised that you're not sure if she's real. Dawn is so pale you can almost see through her. A woman I know calls her a hungry ghost."

"In Asia, the hungry ghosts are the dead whose families disrespected them. They only come out in August."

Slater waved impatiently. "Dawn is the one you met Saturday night in the bar at the Baltimore."

"Who the fuck are you?"

"You don't get to ask the questions. I'm working for Morales. I want to discourage you from paying Dawn. I'm going to put her out of business very soon. Until then, I don't want her to have ready access to capital."

A thin smile played on Goh's lips. "That's very interesting. If she decides to release those photographs, it'll go much worse for your boss than for me, since I had nothing to do with it."

"If those come out, Morales will be indicted, and I'm sure he'd flip on you in a hot minute. Once the jig is up there'd be no point in him protecting you or your investors."

"You're going to put her on ice?"

"Nothing as lurid as that," Slater said.

"So how are you going to shut her down?"

"That's not your concern."

He sighed. "I guess I'll believe it when I see it." Goh rose and stepped around the desk, and stopped in front of him, hands on his hips, and jutted his chin. "Now, get out of my office."

"Why is it that crooks always have zero manners?"

Goh stepped closer and poked him on the shoulder. "You don't get to come into my place and slander me."

Slater slapped his face, left and then right, a rapid kovac. Goh's eyes narrowed, and his mouth became a tight line, and his arm moved in a blur. It was some martial arts technique, and seemed to come from his waist. Slater's head snapped back.

As he stumbled backward, Slater wasn't even sure where Goh had hit him. His nose wasn't bleeding, he found when he touched it, even though it hurt like hell. Maybe he'd actually struck his chin. Whatever he'd done, it had almost knocked him flat.

"Motherfucker," Slater said. "That really, really hurt."

"That is the point."

He rubbed the back of his neck. "Is that from karate?"

"Technically it's hapkido. But there are similar moves in karate."

"You're dangerous, man. It's great that you can be so calm when you're moving. That makes it stealthy."

"If there's nothing else?" Goh gestured to the doorway. "Give my regards to the councilmember."

Slater walked out, through the empty front office, toward the elevators. Even his back hurt. That freaking idiot better not have made him pull something.

On the ride down he did a neck roll, loosening the muscles, trying to shake off the pain. He knew better than to mess with someone who might know martial arts, but he couldn't help himself. That kind of belligerence demanded a kovac.

Walking back to his car, he texted Svetlana:

Can I drop by?

Her reply made him grin:

I am always here for you.

Slater got in the Thunderbird, and pulled into the traffic, and headed toward Glendale.

In front of her building, he climbed out, and paused to stretch his back again, and roll his aching neck. The dirt in the narrow beds between the sidewalk and the wall of the structure had been disturbed, he saw, churned up by a spade, in big alkaline-tinged chunks. It was hard black earth that hadn't grown anything in decades, sterilized by neglect and urban grime.

Walking around to the alley and the entrance, he knew he'd already been identified by the cameras mounted along the roofline. Once he was through the scanner and inside, Svetlana swiveled around on her stool to face him. She was wearing a bright-orange leopard-print top and a red skirt. It was almost like she was intentionally trying to look crazy.

"*Dobraye den,*" Slater said.

"Such lovely pronunciation. Even the saints are smiling."

"You flatter me."

"You look a little green," Svetlana said, her brow furrowing. "Do you need a glass of water?"

"I'm fine. Some idiot punched me in the face this morning."

She nodded. "The perils of our business. So—I just saw you last week. You're becoming a very good customer."

"I'm not sure if you can help me. I need to get a copy of someone's fingerprints, and then transfer them onto another object."

"Obtaining the prints is not so difficult. It's chemistry rather than electronics, but I can help you with it. Transferring them is much more complex. Is this person still alive?"

"Yes," Slater said, and frowned. "Why does it matter?"

"It will work better if you can get new prints on a prepared medium. It's harder to lift existing prints from a bottle or a door handle or a steering wheel."

Slater told her what he was planning in more detail, and Svetlana outlined his options. They finally settled on a technique, and she ran through it with him, all the necessary steps, and he bought the stuff he'd need. Of course she had it all in stock, squirreled away in a storeroom.

"I always feel inspired after talking to you," he said, peeling bills off his wad of cash to pay her.

"This is a very deep compliment," she said. Once she'd tucked the cash away, she eyed him. "You studied gardening and plants, correct?"

His eyebrows shot up. "That's right. I did horticulture at community college."

Slater knew he'd never mentioned that to her, or to her brother. It shouldn't come as a surprise, though, that they would keep close track of their customers, and check into his background. Anyone who bought from them could make serious trouble for their business.

"We need to do something at the front of the building. The city is causing problems. They said our building looks like 'urban decay.'" She waggled her fingers to put the phrase in air quotes. "They don't like the bars on the windows. Can you tell me what to plant there?"

"You want foliage to hide the building?"

"Exactly. It's less disruptive than doing a renovation."

"Well, I saw the soil out front, and it'll need to be replaced," Slater said. "You might have to take out some of the concrete too. There are a few species that you could plant that would grow to cover the facade. I'd say a perennial ivy on the building and a hedge in front of it. Trim it every few months and it'll look beautiful."

"How long will it take to grow?"

"Six months until it has good coverage."

"This would be wonderful. Can you email me

the names of the plants?"

"It would be better to get a professional land-scaper. I can refer someone I know. She could get the soil right. You just have to tell her that your priority is coverage and speed." Slater pulled out his phone. "Let me make sure she's still in the business."

"Your phone won't work in here," Svetlana said. "The building is shielded."

"I'll get her to call you. She's the type who won't ask too many questions."

"Thank you for the introduction. Now I'm the one who's inspired."

Once he was in the alley, he texted a woman he'd gone to school with. She wasn't a lowlife, but she wouldn't be put off by an underworld character like Svetlana.

Climbing into the car, he set his bag of pur-chases on the passenger seat and started the engine, then headed back downtown. It didn't seem smart to be getting involved with Svetlana and her crew on more than a professional level, but it also didn't feel like he had any choice. A while back he'd hooked up with her weird closety nephew, Garik, at Svetlana's insistence, and then he'd managed to find someone else for the guy to obsess over, effec-tively dodging the danger of getting too entwined with the family. But maybe a landscaping referral didn't carry the same kind of risk.

Slater parked at a meter on Los Angeles Street and spent a minute prepping his cell phone, adjusting the settings. He pulled up a photo of some random guy from the web, an athlete with a square jaw.

Next he wiped down the device with his handkerchief, and then holding it by its edges, between his thumb and finger, spritzed liquid onto the screen and the back from one of the little bottles Svetlana had sold him. The stuff smelled sickly sweet, and he cracked the window to dispel the odor, waving the phone in the air to get the stuff to dry.

Climbing out of the car, he kept the device hidden in his palm, cradling it so as not to get his own fingerprints on it. When he walked into the photo studio, Dawn was behind the counter, alone. She frowned when she looked up and recognized him.

"Did you have to lay off all your staff?" he said, waving at the empty room.

"Where's the cash?" she demanded.

"The boss is bringing it to the office today. He'll let me know."

"Losers," she snapped.

"My middle school shrink would have called that labeling," Slater said, his tone calm. "I'm not losing at anything—I'm trying to help you. You'll get your money."

"So what are you doing here now?"

"I wanted to ask you about someone. Do you know this guy?"

Slater handed his phone to her, pressing the power button to illuminate the screen. Dawn peered at it, but the backlight quickly dimmed, just the way he'd set it up. She tapped at the screen to wake it again.

"I've never seen him before. Who is he?"

"Are you sure he's not someone you're squeezing right now?"

Dawn scowled and handed the phone back. "I said I don't know him." Absently wiping her hands together, she added, "Did you spill soda on that thing?"

Slater held the phone by its edges again, folding it inside his hand and out of view. "I think this guy is trying to inject himself into the middle of your grift."

"Impossible. This transaction is between me and Morales. No one else is involved." Her eyes flicked up and down Slater's form. "Except his goon. What does this guy know, and where did you come across him?"

"He runs some porn websites. But that's not for you to worry about." He turned to leave.

"What porn websites?" she demanded, and when he ignored that, she shouted after him, "You'd better be back with my money."

FIFTEEN

❧

SITTING IN HIS CAR again, Slater spritzed the phone with the other chemical Svetlana had sold him, the one to set Dawn's fingerprints. The stuff smelled like window cleaner, and he waved it in the air to dry it off. As the liquid dried, shadowy fingerprints appeared, etched in the sticky material—a beautiful thumbprint on the front, and two others on the back.

Next he pulled a strip of adhesive tape out of the little plastic dispenser Svetlana had provided, and pressed it onto each print, and peeled them off. Holding the tape up to the fading daylight beyond the windshield, he could see the loops and ridges. One of the three was slightly smudged, but overall they were legible, and intact.

Svetlana had also given him a plastic card to temporarily store the prints, and he applied the strips of tape to it, hoping they'd peel off again as promised.

Pocketing the plastic card, he spent a minute rubbing the sticky stuff off his phone, balling it up like old glue. He took a second to reset the screen timeout, and noticed there was a text from Baglio:

Can we talk?

Swiping it away, he checked his tracking map for Conrad's location. Dumbass was at his station, and Slater dialed his cell, glad that he picked up.

"I'm working," Conrad said.

"I find that hard to believe. Wipe the drool off your chin. I have some actual work for you."

He sighed heavily. "What do you need, Slater?"

"Is the Baltimore Hotel in your jurisdiction?"

"You know damn well it's not. It's in Central."

"Even so, there's something there that constitutes a crime."

"If you witnessed a crime, call the police. The number is printed on the side of all the prowl cars."

"It's not really what I'd call an urgent type situation," Slater said. "If you come to check it out, maybe you'll get credit for the bust."

"What kind of crime are you talking about, exactly?"

"I'll show you when you get here."

"Is this some kind of scam?" Conrad demanded.

"Look, I'm just trying to help you out. I promise it'll be worth it."

"I guess I can swing by. Look for me in the lobby."

Slater started the engine, and flicked on his headlights, then drove to the garage under Pershing

Square. From the box he kept in the backseat he grabbed two pairs of black latex gloves and stuffed them into his hip pocket, then walked up to the street and across to the hotel.

Conrad was already standing in the lobby, wearing his uniform. Tall and broad-shouldered, with thick dark hair, his ballistic vest made him look barrel-chested. Such a beautiful man. Turning to look as Slater walked in, he smiled in recognition. He was always so amicable, so pleasant, so laid-back. Why did that grate on Slater's last nerve?

"You shouldn't be loitering here," Slater said, walking up to him. "You're making people nervous."

"Only someone who's up to no good needs to be afraid of the badge."

"It's not about the uniform. It's your hideously ugly face." He gestured toward the hallway. "Come on."

"You're rude, Slater," Conrad said, walking abreast. "There's no other word for it."

"That's not what you said when I had my dick down your throat."

"And crass too. Let's not forget that." He chuckled. "We had some good times, though, didn't we."

"For me it was mostly terror. I think it's called Stockholm syndrome."

Conrad scoffed, and waved his arm. "Where are we going? There's nobody here."

It was true—the ballrooms were all shuttered, and the hallway was empty.

"Men's room," Slater said.

He pushed through the door and glanced around. No one was inside, and he strode over to the little white box mounted low on the wall, next to the row of urinals.

"I happened to notice this device," Slater said, pointing it out. "It's out of place."

"It looks like a motion detector."

"Why is it at waist height?"

"Did you ask the management?"

"I don't think they put it there. I think it's a spy camera."

"What were you doing in here?" Conrad said. "Turning tricks, or just smoking closeted out-of-town businessmen?"

Slater's eyes narrowed. "It's curious that you know about that kind of behavior in such detail."

"Now that you point it out, it does look suspicious." He tapped the box. "The hole there could be a lens."

"If I opened it myself, it would just be my word that I found it here. But you're a sworn officer."

"Let's see what's in it."

Slater pulled out the black latex gloves and handed Conrad a pair.

"You walk around with these in your pocket?" Conrad said, wriggling into them. "Have you been offering spontaneous prostate exams?"

"I brought them to preserve fingerprint evidence. I would have thought you'd run across the concept at some point."

Slater had his gloves on first, and grasped the device, pulling on it. The cover popped off, revealing a green electronic circuit board, and wires, and a cylindrical component attached to the black spot on the front of the case.

Conrad took the little cylinder and peered at it. "This is totally a camera."

On the circuit board Slater saw there was a tiny memory card, and he pulled it from its connector with a fingernail. He had to squint to read what was printed on it.

"It says 256 gigabytes. That's a lot of weenie footage."

Conrad winced. "Oh, man. So much paperwork."

"Go see if there's any more cameras in the stalls."

"Did you see one in the stalls?"

"I didn't check."

He frowned and handed Slater the camera and the plastic housing, then walked toward the row of doors, stepping into the first one and looking around.

Slater turned his back to him and pulled out the plastic card with Dawn's prints on it, then peeled off one of the strips of tape. The print lifted with it, as Svetlana said it would. He pressed it onto the back of the circuit board and rubbed it with his thumb, then pulled the tape off. Examining the board, he could barely see it, but there was definitely a print there now.

The second one he transferred to the inside of the plastic housing, and then he applied the print with the smudge to the back of the case, still stuck to the wall.

Conrad came back, and stood next to him, and put his hands on his hips.

"I don't see anything similar," he said. "But I can't help but think you're up to something."

"All I'm doing is what's called the right thing. Helping the authorities fight crime, and giving you personally a leg up."

With his latex-clad fingers Conrad pried the plastic housing off the wall, leaving a chunk of yellowy double-sided tape. He took the electronics and the memory card from Slater and tucked them inside the white case.

"You should sweep the women's restroom too," Slater said. "And check these pieces for prints."

Conrad frowned. "Great idea, junior detective."

"Do you want to grab dinner? That Thai place you like is near here."

"I can't just leave this—I have to call it in, and write it up, and stand around here waving my arms and talking to the management for three hours, and in the meantime come up with an explanation for why I was so far off my beat. You've basically ruined my evening."

"You should be grateful. You're going to catch a spy-cam pornographer."

"How do you know that's what's going on here?"

"Just a guess."

"What else do you know about this?" Conrad demanded. "Is this about Doris's friend, and that button man?"

"Nothing to do with that. I just don't want video of my dick all over the internet."

"It wouldn't matter—no one would be able to see it. They'd need a magnifying glass."

"Hilarious," Slater said flatly. "There was a time when you worshipped all this." He grabbed his crotch and jutted his chin. "Begged for it."

"I remember things a little differently."

"Listen, you have to leave my name out of this," Slater said, and gestured to the disassembled device in his hand.

Conrad slowly shook his head. "I don't think I can. I have to explain where the tip came from."

"Then spell my name wrong or something. I don't want to be involved."

Slater turned and walked out. Striding through the lobby toward the street, he knew that it had worked. Dick-smack Conrad was too sharp to buy it unquestioningly, and they might summon Slater to come in and make a statement at some point, but there was no doubt now that they'd find Dawn's prints.

As he crossed the dark street toward the square, his phone buzzed in his pants, and he pulled it out to check. Baglio, he saw. Ignoring it, he tucked his phone away and trotted down the stairwell into the garage.

Across the freeway, back in his own neighborhood, he drove to the *pupusería* near his house, and stepped up to order through the grate.

"Two with jackfruit," he told the woman, who greeted him by name. When he paid he overtipped her, like he always did. In that regard, her gift of the statue of Rey Pascual had worked—it had brought her many times more income than the thing was worth.

It was cold out, but he waited on the hard stool out front, elbows on the counter. When the food came he scarfed it down before he headed back to his car.

When he stepped into his apartment a few minutes later, he stopped in his tracks. The little light was on over the stove, and he could see the outline of a figure stretched out on the sofa. As he sat up, he saw who it was—Baglio.

"You broke into my place?" Slater demanded, closing the door behind him.

"It wasn't that hard. It's a cheap-ass lock. Easy to pick."

"That's not the point."

"It makes me think you keep your valuables elsewhere."

"In my office," Slater said.

"Smart." Baglio got to his feet. "Listen, I get that you don't want to see me, but I wanted to talk to you, and I didn't want to wait in the hall like a creep."

"Break-and-enter might fall into that category too."

"I'm sorry for that," he said, and looked away.

"Oh, Baglio—what can I say? I'm not in the market for a boyfriend."

"I know."

"I'm not good for people."

"Neither am I," Baglio said. "That's why I think we're compatible."

Slater sighed. He needed to end this, and end it decisively. Spending time with a guy like this would sink him—pull him deeper into the cesspool. Instead of tracking down lowlifes, he'd turn into one himself.

"Sit down," Slater said, and when Baglio dropped onto the sofa again, he knelt in front of him, and grasped his thighs, and held his gaze. "I can't."

"You don't even want to give it a shot? Just to see what happens. It might turn out to be a train wreck, but we won't know that if we don't try."

"I can't."

"You're sure?" he said carefully.

Slater nodded slowly.

Baglio looked away. "All right. I had to try."

"It's a crush, man. It'll pass."

"I can't just change how I feel."

Slater massaged his thighs. "I understand that. If you want, I can fuck you, since you're already here. But not if that will make things worse for you."

"I'd like that. Maybe it'll help get you out of my system."

Slater pushed his knees apart and reached for his belt, then unzipped his fly, and took him into his mouth. Baglio shifted down to let him get closer, and he quickly got hard, and groaned with pleasure, then put a hand on Slater's cheek to stop him.

"Not here."

Rising to his feet, Slater led him into the bedroom, and got undressed. Baglio unbuttoned his shirt, still watching him with that hangdog look.

Once he had his clothes off, Slater stepped closer and then slapped him, hard enough to turn his head.

"Snap out of it," he demanded.

Baglio's eyes hardened. "It's OK, Slater. I know what you're trying to do."

Slater slapped his other cheek. "So what are you going to do about it?"

Lunging at him, Baglio grabbed his throat, not cutting off his air, but holding tightly enough to maneuver him onto the bed. Slater let him do it, not even feigning resistance. He climbed on top of Slater, straddling him, and lowered his weight onto his pelvis.

"I'm going to teach you a lesson, is what I'm going to do."

Baglio put his hand over his mouth, gently at first. Slater bit into the base of his thumb, making him yelp in surprise, and he clamped his mouth harder, and shifted his weight around on Slater's woody.

Eventually he softened his grip, and Slater took his thumb into his mouth, and sucked on it, holding Baglio's gaze. The guy was breathing hard. Baglio leaned toward the night table to grab a condom, and Slater helped him roll it on. Baglio shifted onto his knees, and repositioned Slater's legs, then pushed into him. Holding his gaze, Slater scowled at him, a tacit challenge. Breathing hard, Baglio drove deeper, and caressed his cheek with his thumb. Slater slapped him hard.

"Damn it," Baglio snapped, and started to pound him.

Slater slapped him again.

"Fuck you," Baglio grunted, and pounded harder. "Fuck you, you fucking lowlife." Increasing the pace, he strained into him. "You fucking psycho." He roared again as he climaxed: "Fuck you."

Sinking onto him, he mouthed his jaw, and Slater felt his hot breath on his neck. Eventually Baglio's breathing slowed, and he rolled onto his side, and grabbed Slater's cock.

"Do you want to do me?"

"Let me fuck you between your legs," Slater said, and grabbed the lube, then climbed on top of him. Meeting his mouth, firm and hot and intent, he lowered his weight onto Baglio's frame, relishing his hot skin as he pumped between his thighs. A minute later he came, and then lay there, his arms around Baglio's head, catching his breath. When he started to drift off, he pulled away and flipped onto his back.

Slater woke later when Baglio turned onto his side and caressed his chest.

"I don't think I deserve you," Baglio said quietly.

He turned to meet his gaze. "I don't know what you're seeing, but it's not me. I'm nothing." Slater waved at the room. "I don't have anything. I do bad things. I'm probably not going to live very long."

"I know how it is. I've done some things. It eats me up sometimes."

Slater thought about that. "If you're going to do that kind of stuff, you have to lean into it. Be OK with it."

"Now you sound like a shrink."

"That's not surprising. I spent half my teenage years sitting in shrinks' offices."

"You were a problem child?"

"I was pissed off a lot."

"I could see that," Baglio said.

Slater turned to him and ran his hand into his hair. "You know that you're more than the bad things you've done."

"You don't know what I've done."

"No one is beyond redemption. You deserve better than me. You deserve to be happy."

Baglio sighed and turned away. Slater listened to him breathing for a while, watched his abdomen rising and falling. Eventually he got up.

"Do you want a drink?" Slater said.

"I want a towel."

He grabbed one in the bathroom and tossed it to Baglio, then went into the kitchen and pulled out the fifth, and guzzled the amber nectar, coughing at the fumes.

When he went back to bed, Baglio wrapped an arm around his chest.

"Is that scotch?"

"Bourbon."

"You smell like Ray's place."

SIXTEEN

D AYLIGHT WAS STREAMING IN the bedroom window when Slater woke. Baglio was on his feet, getting dressed.

"I'm heading out," he said, eyeing Slater. "I won't bother you anymore."

"You never bothered me. I just can't handle the emotional stuff. You'll find someone who can."

Baglio didn't respond to that and heaved a weary sigh. A minute later he'd let himself out. Slater reached for his phone and texted Max:

Baseball?

His reply came soon after:

Let's do it. I'm at the office now.

It was nice not to have a headache, Slater realized, pushing himself out of bed. Once he'd washed up and dressed, he went downstairs to his car and drove out of his neighborhood, across the freeway, through downtown. Pulling into the lot across from their building, he sent Max a text:

I'm in the parking lot.

Max appeared a minute later, strolling out the front entrance and crossing the street. He was wearing his suit, like he always did, as he needed a jacket to cover his weapon. But he wasn't packing today—he'd probably left it in the safe.

Climbing in the passenger door, Max greeted him. "Feeling the need to smash some stuff?"

"You know how it is." Slater pulled into the street and drove a few blocks south, into the industrial zone around the elevated section of the 10 freeway, and nosed through a familiar open gate.

It was a recycling business, and the owner was one of Max's former window-shade clients. The building was a big warehouse with a row of bays for trucks, one with the big door rolled open, a semi-trailer backed up to it.

Slater parked the Thunderbird near the gate, and they walked into the warehouse through a pedestrian door. Not far away a guy in a blue laborer's uniform was driving a forklift, and he stopped as they approached.

"Is Andrés around?" Max asked him.

"Not today," the guy said. "I remember you—you're Max, right?"

"We were going to hit some pots."

"Go for it. You can leave your jacket in the locker room."

Max thanked him, and they went into the staff changing room, where Max hung his suit jacket on a peg. Slater grabbed two pairs of goggles and handed him one as they walked across the big space, past stacks of colorful waste plastic bound in neat bales.

They stepped outdoors into a small yard, with one side open to the main lot where the trucks came and went. Several pallets of stacked-up flowerpots sat against the wall, and the space was littered with pink rubble. Andrés had picked up a container load of these counterfeit terra-cotta pots. They were made of sand and dirt and pink dye, so they didn't work as planters, and they weren't really recyclable—useless for anything besides blowing off steam. Part of the payment Max had negotiated was ongoing access to this place. That worked fine for Andrés because it didn't cost him anything.

"I'll pitch first." Slater picked up the pink-dusted aluminum baseball bat that was propped against the wall and tossed it to Max. At the pallets he grabbed a short stack of the little pots.

"Andrés must be getting over his wife's betrayal," Max said, whiffing the bat around in the air to warm up.

"Why do you say that?"

"Look at all the pots that are still left. He hasn't been out here much."

They both pulled their goggles on, and Max moved a few yards away, and held the bat at the ready, then nodded. Slater tossed a pot to him in a gentle arc. When Max swung at it, he hit it dead on, with a resounding *crack,* turning it into a cloud of dust and rubble that sprayed on the ground.

"Nice," Slater said, and waited for him to get positioned, then tossed another.

Max swung low and split this one in two, the pieces spinning upward and back toward him. He sidestepped out of their path, watching them shatter on the ground.

"Ball one," Max said, and readied the bat again. "So what's going on with your bunco job?"

As he tossed pots, Slater told him about Etta, and Goh, and Baglio. Eventually Max was looking sweaty from all the swinging, and waved for a break.

"So this guy broke into your apartment?" Max said. "That's kind of obsessive. Did you give him a tune-up?"

"Not with my fists."

"OK—that's quite enough detail." Max handed him the bat, then stepped over to the pallets and picked up a handful of pots. "That's not like you— you always keep your dick out of your cases."

"I told you about that, huh." Slater swung the bat around, warming up. He liked the feeling of its heft, the power in it.

"It's a laudable goal," Max said. "Trying to keep some objectivity."

"Thing is, I never actually manage to do it."

Planting his feet, he held the bat at his shoulder and nodded for the pitch. He struck the first one off center, and it shattered on the concrete at his feet.

"You never seem to end up sleeping with your targets," Slater said, repositioning the bat.

Max tossed a pot in a slow arc, and Slater swung hard, turning it into a cloud of dust and detritus with a satisfying *crack*.

"That's because I've got something better waiting."

"That you do. How is Vanessa?" Slater waggled the bat and nodded. "Hit me."

Max talked about her through a couple of pitches, and when he was out of pots, motioned for the bat. Slater surrendered it and went to the pallets to get more.

"So Baglio is just a button man?" Max said. "Does he drop the hatchet too?"

"It's hard to say."

He tossed a pot, and Max smashed it downward, into the concrete.

"I think right now Baglio is a slacker," Slater said, as he waited for the dust to clear. "He doesn't seem to have regular work."

"Neither do we." Max waggled the bat and nodded for another pot.

"It seems to me like you're always doing stuff," Slater said, and pitched a pot, pausing as Max shattered it. "And we always manage to make rent."

They each smashed another stack in turn, and Max told him about the window-shade job he was currently on, following a cheating husband on his evening excursions. Eventually he set the tip of the bat on the ground.

"Enough?"

"We can go," Slater said, and before they stepped inside, they both spent a minute slapping the sandy pink grit off their clothes.

In the locker room Slater hung up the goggles, and Max retrieved his jacket, and they drove back to the office. As they were crossing the street, Slater's phone rang. He pulled it out to check—Conrad.

"What do you want?" Slater said, picking up.

"You had good instincts about that hidden camera you found," Conrad said. "There were two more in the women's restroom. You said there might be. It's almost like you're psychic."

"It's my job," Slater said. "I know what I'm doing. Did you get any prints off the components?"

"Funny you should ask. We did, although the lab said some of the prints were questionable. They had traces of a transfer chemical on them."

"That's so weird."

He stepped onto the elevator with Max. Despite all his efforts, he'd blown it—if the cops decided the fingerprints had been planted, they wouldn't use them against Dawn.

"The good news," Conrad continued, "is that there were prints on one of the cameras in the women's restroom that weren't deemed questionable."

"Who did they belong to?"

"Curiously, all the fingerprints were from the same individual."

Max opened the office door, and Slater followed him inside.

"Have you identified this perp?"

"We picked her up this morning," Conrad said. "She's on parole, so there's no informal interviews or benefit of the doubt."

Slater dropped into the chair behind his desk. "Straight to the hoosegow?"

"That's the procedure. We haven't charged her yet, but it'll happen soon."

"I'm impressed that it went down so fast," Slater said. "Has this been in the news?"

"It might be, eventually," Conrad said. "Sometimes the media doesn't care, but this one has the covert restroom peeping angle, so I bet it'll get some attention."

"Do you know if Dawn made bail?"

"Oh, man—I am not going to pretend you didn't just say the name of the person we picked up. I know I didn't say it."

"You did say it. You just forgot. It's because your IQ is so breathtakingly low. Gaps in your memory are inevitable."

"Fuck you, Slater. How did you know the cameras were connected to Dawn Strezlecki?"

"All right," he said. "Calm down. Off the record—in the course of an unrelated investigation, I found out that Dawn ran some porn websites. When I looked at the content of one of those, I thought the urinals looked familiar, so I went to the Baltimore and spotted what turned out to be that camera. That's when I called you."

Conrad was silent for a moment. "I guess I buy that."

"So did she bail out?"

"Dawn violated her parole. There's no release for her."

"Good to know. Is it possible that she'll walk

because of the questionable fingerprint evidence?"

"A detective here extracted footage from the memory cards that were wired to those cameras," Conrad said. "She did an image search online and found the porn websites you're talking about. They contained a lot of video with the same backdrop, so obviously it was captured by the same camera. The sites are registered to one of Dawn's aliases. But you already knew that."

"It sounds like somebody over there is on the ball."

"So it won't matter if the fingerprint evidence gets thrown out. Dawn is liable for what's on those websites regardless of how the information came to light."

That, Slater thought, was very good news. "Well, I appreciate the heads up."

"Mark it on the wall," Conrad said. "Slater has expressed his appreciation."

"Don't let your head swell up," he said. "You're really just doing what they pay you to do."

Slater ended the call, and found Etta's number, and dialed.

"We need to do some work today," he said when she picked up. "Can you come by my office, pronto?"

"Where's your office?"

"In the Fashion District," he said, and rattled off the address.

"I'm still at school, but I'm done teaching for the day," Etta said. "I can be there in a few minutes. What is it that we need to do?"

"We'll talk when you get here."

Slater ended the call, and a few minutes later, when he heard a sharp knock at the door, he got up to open it.

"I love this building," Etta said, stepping inside. "How wonderful that it's been repurposed for industry."

Her school outfit was a big shift from the homeless drag she'd worn on Saturday—today she had on a sharp dark jacket and gray trousers.

"I've been here a while," Slater said, "and you're the first person to say that."

She gestured to the statue on the front desk. "Hey—that's Rey Pascual."

"You must go to the same church as my *pupusa* vendor. It was a gift from her."

"It's a very cute rendering of him."

Max stepped into his office doorway, pulling on his jacket. Slater introduced them, and explained that Max was his business partner.

"What's with the *pistola*?" Etta said, gesturing to his weapon.

"I'm a private investigator," Max said. "It's part of the job."

"A real PI. How cool is that?"

"That's refreshing," Max said. "Most people think PIs are sleazy."

"It's totally cool," she said. "You get to shoot people."

Max laughed as he adjusted his lapels. "I try not to. Although using it as a deterrent is definitely pie."

"What does that mean, 'it's pie'?"

He raised his eyebrows. "What's the best part of dinner?"

Etta nodded. "The pie."

"You're definitely one in a million," Slater said. "No one else knows who Rey Pascual is, and no one ever thinks this building is cool, and no one thinks Max is cool."

"Hey," Max said, and shot him a look.

"It sounds like you two should get out more," Etta said.

"On my way," Max said, stepping past them to the front door. "Etta, you're a keeper."

"Can I borrow the Courier?" Slater said.

Max flashed a palm as he opened the door. "My pickup is your pickup."

Once he'd gone, Etta said, "How great is it to have a partner like that? My girlfriend won't even let me drive her car. Like, ever."

"What's her ride?"

"It's a crummy little VW."

"We can talk in my office," Slater said, and led her inside. He dropped into his chair and waited for her to sit on the other side of the desk.

"So what's going on?" she said.

"I found out that Dawn is selling footage of people in public restrooms on a porn website."

"That's disgusting."

"She got arrested this morning."

"You turned her in?"

"Indirectly," Slater said.

"How do they know it was her?"

"I made sure her prints were on one of the cameras. More importantly, the porn domains are registered under her name." He gestured vaguely. "It's a long story."

"Do you think she's going away?" Etta said, her brow furrowing.

"She's on parole, so it's worse than it would be for a civilian. She'll be in for a while. Maybe until her trial."

Etta slapped her leg and cackled. "We did it."

"We're not finished. You and I need to go clean out her apartment, and then her office. The cops will get there eventually. We need to get ahead of them."

"The blackmail photos."

"If she's really shrewd, she might have copies off-site—on a thumb drive locked in a bank deposit box or hidden in her mama's attic. But they also might only be on her computer or stashed in her pad."

"Why do you need me?"

"It'll go faster with two sets of eyes. I thought you said you wanted to do something. Take action, you said."

"So let's roll." Etta got up and stepped into the front office.

Slater had to grin at her enthusiasm as he followed her out. He flicked off the lights and twisted his key to bolt the door as they left. Once they were across the street in the parking lot, Etta gestured to a little red Prius C.

"Do you want me to drive?"

"I'm driving," Slater said. "Can two people even fit in that thing?"

"It's roomier than it looks."

"It's cute, at least."

"It's not supposed to be cute. It's supposed to be practical."

"Beep-beep," Slater said.

"You're a car chauvinist."

He got in behind the wheel of the Thunderbird and reached across to unlock the passenger door for her.

"This thing is the opposite of practical," she said, climbing in. "What does it get—like, four miles to the gallon? Do you order your spare parts from the ancient history museum?"

"It goes like a bat out of hell," Slater said, and pulled into the street.

"So why do we need your partner's pickup?"

"We're going to pose as plumbers to get into Dawn's pad. Plumbers show up in a truck, not a beautiful classic Thunderbird."

"Why plumbers? Why not the cable company, or the gas company?"

"Those businesses have recognizable logos on their vehicles and their uniforms. Plumbers could look like anybody. And with plumbers, nobody wants to get too close to your work. They always assume it's about malfunctioning sewer lines."

"Good point." Etta eyed him. "It sounds like you've done this before."

On Bunker Hill, Slater pulled up to the underground garage of Max's building, and dug in the glove box for the remote opener.

"That guy lives here?" Etta said. "It's so bougie."

"It's also near half a dozen freeways," Slater said, waiting for the gate to open. "These buildings are full of judges and politicians, so security is tight. There's always cops around."

"I guess I should feel some solace that my tax dollars are protecting the instruments of the state."

"You sound like a dissident," Slater said, eyeing her as he nosed into the garage. He pulled into the stall beside Max's little green pickup and killed the engine.

"Now, this is cute," Etta said, stepping out and looking it over.

"It's also practical," Slater said. "Get in."

Revving the tinny little engine, Slater drove the pickup to Westlake, and turned into his alley, and pulled into his garage. As the door rolled down, he went to the shelves with his gardening stuff and found a pair of dark blue coveralls.

"Will these fit you?" he said, tossing them to Etta. "They're baggy on me."

"I'm not that big," she said, scowling at him.

A minute later she'd taken off her jacket, and stepped into them, and rolled up the sleeves. They were snug around her hips but didn't look uncomfortable. Slater put on his own pair, and then pulled on a ball cap.

"We look so blue-collar," Etta said, looking him over. "I'd buy it."

Past the nose of the truck stood Slater's armored cabinet, and he stepped over to open it. Built to look like a cheap office-supply storage cupboard, it was really an oversize safe hidden in plain view. This was where he kept all his illicit tech—essentially everything he bought from Svetlana.

Today he pulled out the lock reader and the key binder that went with it, and loaded them into a red plumber's toolbox. The reader was a small probe the size of a key with a cable to connect it to his phone, but the binder was heavy, with dozens of pages of little pouches containing hundreds of keys.

"What is that stuff?" Etta said, watching him as he closed the cabinet.

"Our ticket into the grifter's house." He carried the toolbox to the truck bed and set it inside the cargo box. "Let's go."

They both got into the little pickup, and Slater backed into the alley, checking his phone for Dawn's address as he waited to make sure the garage door rolled all the way down. He copied it into his navigation app and set the phone on the seat between them.

"It's not far."

"How do you know where she lives?"

"It was on her rap sheet." Slater glanced at her. "When you're incarcerated or on parole, a lot of your privacy goes out the window."

Minutes later they were in Dawn's neighborhood.

"This must be Echo Park," Etta said, gazing out the side window.

"It's Angeleno Heights."

"I'm pretty sure it's Echo Park."

"And I know it's Angeleno Heights." Slater pulled over to the curb. "It's that building. Unit D."

"It looks like one of those old studio garden apartments."

"That's good for us—it means there's no gate and no doorman. And the units look tiny, so there won't be a roommate."

"Dawn's definitely in jail?"

"I heard it from a cop."

They climbed out, and Slater pulled his ball cap low over his brow. As Etta stepped around the back of the truck, he handed her a pair of latex gloves, then put on his own.

"No prints?" she said, wriggling her hands into them.

"Leave no trace," he said quietly, glancing around, and then pulled the red toolbox out of the cargo compartment. "When we get to her door, I'm going to squat for a minute to get it open. You stand with your back to me, and if you see anyone, you start talking."

"And say what?"

"It doesn't matter. It's a signal to me that we're being observed."

This style of cottage apartment had been built as film studio housing a century ago, and they still dotted the central part of the city. This one looked typical: a row of tiny stucco cottages with terra-cotta tile roofs instead of shingles.

Slater walked into the courtyard. There were a few patio chairs, and a metal table with an ashtray on it, but nobody was around. The space was lush with succulents, including a stand of orange pencil tree. That was a stupid thing to plant in a place where people hung out. The sap would burn your skin—if someone inadvertently broke off a branch, they could wind up in the hospital.

There were four units on either side, and D was at the far end. Striding up to the door, Slater set down his toolbox and banged on the wood with the heel of his fist.

"Maintenance," he called.

Listening closely, there was no response, no sound of movement within. The keyhole above the handle bore the logo of a standard mass-produced lock. That was a good sign—the probe couldn't read anything too exotic. It was one of Svetlana's very effective but very illegal tools, and he pulled it out of the plumber's box and plugged the cable into his phone.

Svetlana's app popped up on the screen with the message "готов." He had no idea what the word was, but he knew it meant he could start. Gently sliding the slender probe into the keyhole, the screen flashed green and showed two numbers: 119, and below it, 121. Pulling the binder out of the toolbox, he flipped through the heavy pages and slipped the keys with those numbers out of their pouches.

Glancing over her shoulder, Etta spoke under her breath. "Where did you get that?"

"Don't ask," he said, briefly scanning the courtyard.

The first key slid into the lock, but it wouldn't

budge the bolt. When he tried the second one, it twisted freely, unlocking the door with a soft *thunk*.

Slater quickly loaded the binder into the toolbox, then picked it up and stepped inside. The room was dark.

"Hello," he called loudly, just to be sure.

"No alarm," Etta said quietly, closing the door behind them.

"Rentals don't usually have one," Slater said, and flicked on the room lights, and surveyed the space. A sofa and a side table and a small desk took up most of the room, with a kitchen counter at the back.

"At least she's tidy."

"Just like her studio. It makes our work easier." He pointed to the back of the apartment. "You start in the bedroom. I'll work out here."

"What am I looking for?" she said, pushing up the sleeves of her coveralls.

"Electronic storage. Hard drives or thumb drives or memory cards. Look everywhere, but put stuff back. We don't want it to look like it's been searched."

Etta went to the bedroom, and Slater started digging through the bookcase. There were only a dozen or so books, and he flipped through each, and gave them a shake, then set them back. He looked under the sofa cushions, and then lifted the sofa to look under it, and under the coffee table.

There was nothing relevant in the top drawer of the little desk, or under it, but in the lower one was a soft makeup bag with six rolls of film in it. Slater opened a couple of the containers. It was the same kind of film he'd taxed from Dawn at the hotel and from Marty on the street. He zipped the bag closed again and dropped it into his plumber's toolbox.

Next he looked behind the TV and felt under the TV cabinet, then checked the fridge and the kitchen drawers. Etta stepped out of the bedroom.

"I found this." She held up a thin memory card stuck to a piece of adhesive tape.

"Where was that?"

"Taped to the back of the lamp beside her bed."

"Good work. I hope it's the only one. Did you check the bathroom?"

"Nothing in there," Etta said. "What did you find?"

"Six rolls of old-school film. It's what Dawn gives some of her blackmail victims when they pay up."

Etta frowned. "Why?"

"She says it's nice to have something tangible to take home."

"She's a damn sociopath."

"Max called her an artisanal grifter." He looked around. "I think we're done here—let's go."

He followed her into the courtyard and set down the toolbox for a moment to lock Dawn's front door. Standing in front of the next apartment was a gray-haired guy wearing a plaid sweater. A grocery bag dangled from one hand, and a set of keys were poised in the other, but he hesitated at his door, watching them. Etta moved a few paces away, and Slater ignored the guy until he spoke.

"Were you in Dawn's apartment?"

Slater affected a slight Spanish accent. "We were fixing the plumbing."

"Who gave you the key?"

He looked to Etta. "Do you remember her name? Was it Snowball?"

"Maybe Snowplow?" Etta said, knitting her brow.

"Pale as a ghost." Slater tucked the key away and picked up his toolbox.

"Hair like dry straw," Etta offered. "You know how it looks when you max out on the peroxide."

"How could Dawn have given you her key?" the guy said. "The police were here first thing this morning. They took her away."

"She's undocumented?" Etta said.

"I don't know about the police," Slater said. "The blond came by my shop yesterday. Her sewer line backed up." He waggled the fingers of his free hand as if they were wet. "That apartment needs to air out for a day or two."

The guy's nose wrinkled in disgust.

"What was she arrested for?" Slater said.

"I have no idea. They weren't in the regular uniform, but their big heavy vests said POLICE on them. They came in with their guns drawn."

Slater shrugged and followed Etta out to the street. As they approached the little pickup, Etta glanced back at the courtyard.

"Is he watching us?" Slater said quietly, stowing the toolbox.

"Nope."

"Excellent. That means he bought it."

SEVENTEEN

ᔕᔕᔕᔕᔕᔕᔕᔕᔕᔕ

CLIMBING IN AND REVVING the engine, Slater popped the clutch and pulled into the street.

"Do you think it's significant that there was no computer in her place?" Etta said.

Braking for a red light, Slater eyed her. She was good at this. "You're right. Everyone has a computer."

"Maybe it's at her shop."

"Let's go find out."

Cruising downtown and onto Los Angeles Street, Slater found an open meter almost in front of Dawn's studio. The heavy metal shutter was down—the place was locked up.

He carried the toolbox to the entrance and dropped to one knee, leaning close to the lock on the shutter to insert the probe. Without even being told, Etta shielded him by standing with her back to him. Svetlana's app told him what key to use, and a moment later he had it out of the binder, and tried it in the lock.

"Yes," Slater said softly as the key twisted easily and unlocked it. He rolled the metal partway up and then tried the same key in the studio's front door. It worked, and he pushed the door open, ducking under the bottom of the shutter. Etta followed him in and then bolted the door.

"She doesn't have an alarm here either," she said.

"No alarm and no security cameras. It's smart not to have them when your business is extortion." He gestured to the cash register. "Her staff weren't in on the grift, so there won't be anything in the till. But have a look under the counter."

Slater stepped into Dawn's office and dug through the file cabinet. It wasn't locked, and there didn't seem to be anything but paperwork and some photos. His latex gloves made quick work of riffling through the files.

Digging in her desk drawers, he found another film container, and tucked it in his pocket. Etta stepped in.

"I went through the work room," she said. "Lots of photography supplies but nothing electronic."

"Dawn's laptop is here," he said, gesturing to it on the desktop. "I'll have to take it. I should be able to find someone who can break into it."

"I can get into it," she said, and stepped around the desk to sit, then flipped open the computer.

"How are you going to do that?"

"Dawn was a little sloppy when I was in here one

day. She assumed I couldn't see her key in her password. It's a stupid one—I could see it from across the desk." On the keyboard she typed 5-5-5-4.

"That worked?"

"I'm in," Etta said, and shifted closer.

"You could totally work in my business," Slater said.

She scoffed, not looking at him.

"Seriously—you're good at this. You're totally calm. Most people would be nervous about what we're doing. When you get nervous you make mistakes."

"If I can handle a room full of teens with raging hormones," she said, "I can handle a break-and-enter. Plus eighth-graders are every bit as devious as Dawn Snowden."

Slater moved to watch over her shoulder as Etta clicked through the computer's files.

"This might be something," she said. "It's in a cloud drive. The folder is called 'Public Weenie.' They're all video files."

She clicked on one, and it popped up to reveal a man stepping up to a urinal in the familiar hotel men's room, then unzipping his fly.

"Ew," Etta snapped, and quickly closed the video.

"Those are from the hidden camera she planted."

"Was she blackmailing these guys?"

"She was selling this footage on her porn sites. Blackmailing my client was accidental. Her weenie cam caught him in an illicit meeting."

"Should I delete all this?"

"Let's leave that for the cops to find. It'll help nail her."

Etta clicked around some more. "This folder is called 'Money.' Doesn't that sound like blackmail stuff? These are all still images."

When she clicked on one of the files, the image was of the man and woman in the restroom stall, one of the photos on the roll Slater had taken from Marty. Opening a second one revealed the woman with an ecstatic expression on her face as the man mouthed her breasts.

"Straight people are nuts," Etta muttered.

She scrolled farther down the folder and clicked on another image. It was one of Baglio with Morales.

"I know that guy," Etta said. "Isn't he on city council? What's he doing with all that cash?"

"Maybe you should forget you saw that one."

"So that's your client." Etta sat back. "I won't ask. Should I copy all these?"

"Do you want that video of you floating around?" Slater demanded. "No copies means no one else can use these to chisel people."

"You're right. We delete it all?"

"Nuke it."

Etta spent a minute deleting files in the cloud drive, selecting photos and folders, clicking through the warnings.

"Make sure you empty the trash folders too," Slater said.

"I know how this works," she said, and frowned. "Just let me make sure there are no local copies." A moment later she folded the laptop closed. "And we're done."

"Can you write down that password? It'll save the cops some work."

Opening Dawn's top drawer, she found a sticky yellow notepad and scrawled "PIN: 5554" on it, then peeled off the note and pressed it onto the top of the computer.

"Maybe put it underneath," Slater said. "That way it might look like Dawn wrote it herself."

"You should have brought some red ribbon," Etta said, peeling the note off and sticking it on the desktop under the computer. She rose and pushed Dawn's chair under her desk. "You could have tied it all up with a lovely bow for them."

Once they were out on the street, Slater set his toolbox down and locked the door, then pulled down the shutter. A guy stood a few paces away, watching them, but from the look of his grubby clothes he was homeless, and his glazed eyes implied that he was high, or unmedicated, or otherwise out of it, and so not really a threat.

"How you doing?" Etta called to him.

The guy mumbled something incoherent and turned away.

Once he'd locked the shutter, Slater lifted the plumber's box into the bed of the Courier, then climbed into the cab and peeled off his gloves.

Etta did the same, then said, "We did it, man— hit me up top."

Slater slapped her palm, grinning as she hooted in celebration.

"You can't tell anyone what we did today. Not even your girlfriend. It's a whole laundry list of felonies." He started the engine and revved it as he pulled into the street.

"I get why it's illegal. It feels so damn good."

"There's no guarantee that Dawn doesn't have backups," Slater said. "And it's possible that we missed something."

"Still, it'll slow that albino down."

"Hopefully she'll be in the big house for a while. That'll have the same effect."

"What about Marty?"

"He might have copies of some of the stuff," Slater said, "but I think he'll be too afraid to put the bite on anyone with Dawn sitting in jail. If you hear from him, you call me, and we'll deal with him."

Up on Bunker Hill, he pulled into Max's garage again and parked beside the Thunderbird. Climbing out, he peeled off his coveralls.

"What are you going to do with the film, and that memory card?"

"Let's trash them right now."

Opening the plumber's box, he pulled out the bag of film canisters and handed her one. He tipped a roll out of its can and pried the end off with his fingernail, then pulled out the spool of film, letting it coil around his hand.

"Before it's processed," he said, "whatever images were on the film get destroyed by exposure to light."

Etta took hold of the end of the strip and studied it. "It's such a weird color. Not quite brown, not quite green. It smells weird too. Like chemicals."

"Help me out here." He dug in the bag for another one and pried it open.

Soon they had all of them open and exposed, with a messy pile of coiled film on the concrete floor between them. Slater held up a strip to look at it against the light fixture, just to make sure, but it was foggy and blank.

"Dawn had a point," Etta said. "It's cathartic to destroy the physical version. Way more satisfying than just deleting digital files."

Next Slater peeled the tape off the little memory card and snapped it in half.

"Do you see a sewer drain?" he said.

Etta took a few steps past the Courier. "Over here."

Slater squatted and dropped the remnants of the card through the grate in the floor.

"The film can just go in the trash," he said. "It's useless now."

Once he'd lifted the plumber's box into the trunk of the Thunderbird, and piled the coils of film in with it, they both climbed in. He drove out into the waning daylight and headed toward his office.

"Listen," Slater said, eyeing Etta sidelong. "You need to get away from those perverts you work for."

"That's not how most people conceptualize the church."

"They choose not to have sex and then micromanage your sex life. That's a textbook definition of perversion."

Etta sighed and looked out at the city rolling by. "I like the kids."

"I know someone who was in public education for a long time. When you work for a normal school board, you can eat all the pussy you want, and no one cares."

"Nice," she said flatly.

"And I'm sure they have the same kind of mouthy obnoxious kids as in Jesus land. She's been out of the game for a while, but she'll have some job ideas. Her name is Doris. I'll text you her phone number."

In the parking lot across from his building, Slater pulled up beside the red Prius, and left the engine running.

"You're not going into your office?" Etta said.

"I've got one more thing to do."

She popped open the door, but hesitated. "I don't know how to thank you. You set me free from that parasite. Probably a lot of other people are free of her now too."

"You freed yourself," Slater said. "You're the one who had a way to get into her cloud storage."

Etta nodded. "Thanks, man."

Once she'd climbed out, he nosed back into the traffic, and drove a few blocks to Spring Street, and parked near Marty's building. Pulling out his phone, he dialed Marty's number, and when he picked up, Slater affected an amicable tone.

"I'm the guy who found your phone the other day. I might have found something else of yours."

"Like what?" Marty demanded.

"I picked up an old-school roll of film. It was a few steps from your little bag. Is that yours?"

"Damn it—I asked you specifically about what you found. You told me there wasn't anything else."

"I guess I forgot," Slater said. "But I found this in my jacket, and then I remembered you. It's a little yellow roll with '100' written on it. Do you want it back?"

"You idiot. Of course I want it back."

"I'm right near your building. What unit are you in? I can bring it up."

"It's 1260. I'll give the concierge your name. What was it again?"

"John Slade," he said, and ended the call.

It seemed pretentious to have a concierge, Slater thought, climbing out of his car, when these apartments weren't high-end at all. More likely it was just a doorman. Being on the edge of Skid Row like this, they likely needed some level of security. The woman on the front desk was polite, and checked for his pseudonym on her computer, then pointed him to the elevators. As he knocked on Marty's door, he held his phone at the ready, and when the guy pulled it open, he took a photograph of him.

"What are you doing?" he demanded. Marty was wearing tan chinos and a blue sweater, and had some dark-red stubble on his face.

"I was thinking about what you said." Slater put a hand on the door and stepped in, and Marty took an involuntarily step back.

The place had Berber carpeting, and a bland

puffy living room set, and a big TV on the wall. Across the room was a sliding glass door leading out to a balcony.

"What are you talking about? What did I say?"

"The way people pay you to keep their genitals out of public view." He closed the door behind him. "What did you mean by that?"

"That's none of your damn business. Where's my film?"

"I don't have it on me."

"You just said that you'd bring it." He frowned. "Do you want money? Is that it? I can give you twenty dollars."

Slater guffawed. "You're a piece of work, brother. What do you call something that's lower than a lowball?"

"You don't get to laugh at me." Puffing out his chest, Marty stepped closer. "You don't know who I am. I can fuck you up so bad."

Slater planted a palm on his chest and shoved him backward, farther into the apartment.

"I know exactly who you are."

"You can't push me around." Marty balled his fists. "I'm warning you. I studied savate with the top instructor in Brussels. I'm very skilled at it."

"Is that the French kickboxing thing? Man, even your combat skills are bougie."

Watching him pose, it was clear Marty had no idea what he was doing. His fists were squeezed so tight that his knuckles were white. Putting so much pressure into them made them ineffective as weapons—he'd break his hand if he hit anything too hard.

"Where's my film?" Marty demanded.

"So what's the deal with you and Dawn and the porn sites?"

His expression shifted, and he straightened up. "How do you know about Dawn?"

"I know you manage the websites for her. But how involved are you?"

"She told you that?"

"Does she put up the hidden cameras, or do you?"

"Who the fuck are you?" Marty demanded, raising his voice.

"I've had some business dealings with Dawn." Slater gestured casually. "I know she's the mastermind, and you're the flunky, correct? You don't seem smart enough to be in charge."

"Fuck you," he spat. "You fucking loser. I put up most of those cameras myself. It was my idea to squeeze the idiots who had sex in the stalls, or went in there to shoot up."

"Drugs?" Slater said, raising his eyebrows.

"You'd be amazed how many otherwise functional people are on injectables." He waved his arms. "And if you don't want your wife to know you're sleeping around, don't fuck someone else in a public restroom."

"I understand the business model," Slater said. "But why were her fingerprints on the cameras, and not yours?"

"We both wore gloves, dummy. Nobody's prints were on them." He frowned. "Wait—how do you know all this?"

Clearly Marty hadn't heard yet that Dawn had been popped this morning. Slater put his hands on his hips and jutted his chin.

"I could explain it to you, but I don't think you'd be able to understand."

Marty pressed his mouth into a tight line. Slater knew what was coming next—the guy wasn't actually trained to fight, and his shoulder dipped as he wound up, and then lunged at him with a wild right hook. Slater leaned away to avoid the blow, in his periphery watching his hand flail at the air past his ear, and then he struck Marty hard, aiming for the cheekbone rather than the jaw or the nose, so that he wouldn't break anything or draw blood. Marty's head spun, and his body followed, and he fell to his hands and knees on the carpet, dazed.

Slater looked around for cameras. An egomaniac like this might just record the minutiae of his mundane life, but he couldn't see any. It was kind of a basic apartment for a self-proclaimed famous artist, with a little round dining table, and blankets draped on the sofa, and a cheap countertop separating the living room from the kitchen.

Bending over him, Slater put his hands in his armpits and dragged Marty to the balcony door, and slid it open, hauling him out into the looming twilight. A pair of dusty patio chairs sat out here, along with some kind of perennial *Salvia* in a terra-cotta pot, but there wasn't anything else, allowing easy access to the railing. This apartment was at the back of the complex, he saw, not on the street side, so the view was of the back of an office building and a parking structure. That worked better—there would be fewer witnesses.

Marty was starting to return to lucidity, and Slater lifted him under his arms to heave his butt up onto the railing, positioning him there and then holding his ankles.

"Whoa," Marty shouted, realizing where he was as he straightened up. "Put me down."

Slater leaned into him, pushing his chest with his forehead, and he lost his balance, clawing at Slater's head but falling backward, his butt slipping over the edge until just his knees were notched over the rail. Marty screamed and flailed his arms as he struggled to get back up. In the fading light, far below, Slater could see a patch of lawn and a concrete walkway leading to the parking structure.

After he'd flailed for a moment, Slater grabbed his collar and pulled Marty partway up.

"You're going to show me the photos."

"You psycho," he shouted, and swatted at Slater's face. "Let go of me."

"Are you sure that's what you want?" Swatting away his fist, Slater shoved him over again, letting him hang in midair, shouting unintelligibly. "It's almost dark out, Marty. Do you want it to be lights out for you too?"

The guy was heavier than he looked, and all the panicky squirming made it harder to maintain his grip, but Slater held firm to his ankle, and kept his other shin pinned with his body.

Once he'd grabbed a fistful of Marty's sweater

and pulled him partway up again, Slater said, "Now, what are you going to show me?"

"Whatever you want. Just pull me up." His eyes bulged, and his face was bright red. "Pull me up," he shouted.

Slater lifted him up again, and once his butt was on the rail, Marty hurled himself forward, landing on all fours on the concrete floor of the balcony. The guy was panting, and disheveled now, his shirt untucked and his sweater askew.

"You're a fucking psycho," he spat.

"I know. Where's your computer?"

As Marty stood up, Slater grasped the back of his collar with one hand, a tacit warning not to do anything unexpected. Stepping into the bedroom, to his computer desk, Marty shrugged him off and sat down.

This wasn't any roomier than Slater's bedroom. It certainly didn't align with him being a public figure, a famous person, a lauded artist. That narrative had to be some kind of self-deception.

The desk was shoved up against the wall at the foot of his bed, with a flatbed scanner at one end, and a negative scanner like the one Olivia had sold him. Piled on top of the components was the body of an SLR camera attached to another electronic device. That must be what Marty used to transfer the digital images onto film.

Marty was still breathing hard as he pulled open his laptop. He clicked through a stack of files and brought up a video of the urinals in the hotel men's room.

"Not that bullshit," Slater said. "The blackmail photos."

Marty huffed and clicked around until a little notification window popped up, with an angry red exclamation mark and a message:

Shared folder not found.

"That's weird," he muttered.

"Dawn shared the images with you in a cloud drive?"

"She's the one who always pulled the video off the cameras, so she's the file owner." He sat back. "All this is about her. It's nothing to do with me. I helped her once in a while with tech support."

"That's not what you said a minute ago," Slater said, studying his face. It didn't really matter, he decided. The prosecutors would decide how involved Marty was, and what was going to happen to him.

"Did you keep any local copies of the photos?" Slater said.

"It's all in Dawn's cloud folders. I don't know why she cut off my access to those images but not to the website videos."

Slater stepped away, toward the bedroom door. "You need to stop blackmailing people."

"You're a goddamn bully," Marty said, twisting in his chair and scowling at him. "You don't get to tell me what to do."

It was amazing how irrational this guy was— Slater could easily dangle him over the balcony railing again. But there was no point in doing that now. He'd found out what he needed.

Once he was downstairs, he walked out to the street, ignoring the concierge as he went past. With any luck this place was busy enough that she wouldn't remember his face. Marty was so deluded that he might try to go after him, and call the cops, and whine to them: "Oh, poor me. He hung me over the balcony rail." But Marty would have his own problems to deal with once they connected him to the porn sites. Slater had no idea what the law was around filming people naked without their permission, but it was definitely illegal.

Climbing into the Thunderbird, Slater looked at his phone, and dialed Doris.

"I think I'm hallucinating," she said when she answered. "You've called me twice in a week."

"We need to talk. Can you meet me for dinner?"

"Can I bring Albert?"

"It's business. Tell him to take the night off, and go inhale some ether, or whatever it is that he does recreationally besides mooch off you."

"He's not a drug user," Doris said flatly.

"You can't be completely sure of that. Doctors can get all the dope they want."

Doris sighed impatiently. "How about that Mexican place on Sunset? They have some of your vegan food."

Once he'd ended the call, Slater flicked on the headlights and drove a few blocks to Andy's place. He parked in a street space out front and fed some coins into the meter.

When Andy answered the door, Slater followed

him into his loft. Andy turned to him, and he slid his hands around his waist, and met his mouth. They spent a minute that way, in the warm intensity of it, and Slater felt his dick tighten in his jeans. Eventually he pulled away.

"You're getting me wound up."

"If that's not why you're here, it means this … is a work visit," Andy said, and dropped into his desk chair.

"Can you put a photo online without it being traceable?"

"You mean on social media sites?"

"I don't care where, as long as it gets eyeballs and people can copy and share. Maybe some gossip sites, or porn commentary sites. Is that a thing? The key is that it can't be traced back to me, or to you."

Andy nodded. "I can probably do that. What photos?"

"Just one." He pulled out his phone and found the picture he'd just taken of Marty, standing in the doorway of his apartment, his brow furrowed. "I'm texting it to you. What's most important is the caption. I want the cops to find this when they look for this guy, or look for the websites he runs."

"What's the caption?"

"Something like, 'This is the guy who runs Public Cooch and Public Weenie.'"

"He works with Dawn?"

"For her, or with her, I'm not sure which. The prosecutors can sort it out."

"What are they going to … prosecute him for?"

"All the footage was illegally obtained. Those

aren't actors. They're people using public restrooms for real."

"The whole thing is so … gross. Do you want to … put his name with the image?"

"Great idea—it's Marty Gregson."

"Text me that." Andy leaned back in his chair. "I can't guarantee that the police or the prosecutors will see it, but I can put it out there."

"You're the best."

"I know. And it's going to cost you."

"Send me an invoice," Slater said flatly. "I have to go."

"Bye, hot stuff," Andy called after him.

Walking out to his car, his phone buzzed in his pants. When he pulled it out, he saw that it was Baglio.

"Are you inside my apartment right now?" Slater said when he picked up.

"Ouch. I guess I deserve that. I'm actually at my friend's place, where I've been staying. I'm packing up—I found a job opportunity in New York."

"That was quick."

"Yeah, well, I've been at loose ends for a while now. It's a gig with a business that my cousin runs. It'll give me a change of scenery. A fresh start. To clear my head, you know?"

"Is it something you can stomach?"

"I think so," Baglio said. "Debt collection, but in the legit sector, so no strong-arm stuff."

"Well, one thing I know about New York is that there's tons of guys."

"I just wanted to say good-bye."

"I know you're going to be OK," Slater said, climbing into his car.

"I know. Anyway—look me up if you ever get over there."

Slater sat behind the wheel for a while after he ended the call. There was a lump in his throat. That made no freaking sense—it wasn't his fault that the guy got crushed out on him. He had no reason to feel sticky about it.

EIGHTEEN

A T HIS APARTMENT SLATER saw that the tumblers had been put away, and his bed was made—Rosa had been here. He took the time to shave and put on a clean shirt, one of the ones Rosa had ironed for him, and then pulled on his faux leather jacket. It wasn't really equivalent to getting dressed up, but there was no need for Doris to think he was more of a ruffian than she already did.

Flicking on his headlights, he drove up to Sunset and parked in the lot behind the restaurant Doris had picked, then walked inside. The place was busy, and noisy, with a small crowd at the desk waiting for tables, and lots of bodies in the bar. Slater walked over to it, surveying the room, but Doris wasn't here yet.

Elbowing his way to the bar, he leaned in and nodded to the bartender, a fresh-faced guy with dark hair. When he approached, Slater asked him for a Corona, then set a sawbuck on the bar top. In his jeans his phone rang with an irritating familiar ringtone: *No wire hangers! What's wire hangers doing in this closet when I told you no wire hangers—ever?*

"I'm inside waiting for you," he said when he picked up.

"And I'm looking right at you," Doris said. "My handsome son."

He looked around the bar, but couldn't see her in the crowd.

"You know," she said, "it warms my heart to see people admiring your cute little butt."

"Good god, woman," Slater thundered.

"I'm just saying. You have lots of options, and in a wide array of genders."

"Where are you?"

"At a table. Eight o'clock."

Slater looked in that direction and finally spotted her, sitting in the shadows near the wall, at a table for two wedged in among several others. She already had a margarita in front of her. Once he had his beer in hand, he carried it over and leaned in to kiss her hello, then pulled off his jacket and hung it on the back of his chair. As he sat across from her, the waitress stepped up, clad in a festive frilly dress in a surreal shade of fuchsia. He'd forgotten about that—this place was old-school, and they still had some of the 1940s touches.

"Do you want to look at the menu?" she asked.

"I know what I want," Slater said, and he and Doris both ordered.

Once the waitress had left, Doris eyed him. "So what's so urgent that you needed to see me tonight?"

"I have a moral dilemma."

"Explain," she said, and sipped her margarita.

"The primary rule in my business is that my loyalty has to be to the person who hired me. Even if they're crooked, or continually lie to my face."

"That's a good rule. You want to be able to depend on the people you hire."

"And you don't want people like me to switch allegiance to someone who offers more money." Slater shifted in his chair. "In a way, you hired me, don't you think? If I can make myself believe that, I can wiggle out of my obligation to Morales."

"I don't like the sound of this. What did you find out?"

"First, which is it? You hired me, or he did?"

"I got you into this," Doris said firmly. "Now tell me what's going on." She held up a finger. "Just the facts—no spin, and no soft-sell, and no sugarcoating."

The waitress stepped up with their plates and set them on the table.

"Let's eat first," he said.

Slater made quick work of his broccoli and bell pepper fajitas, and Doris ate a third of her enchilada before she set her fork down.

"So spill it," she said.

"I'll let the photos do the explaining."

Slater pulled out his phone and found the images of Baglio giving the cash to Morales, then handed it to her. He eyed the people at the tables on either side of her, sitting close enough to see the screen if they wanted to, but neither of them was paying any attention. As Doris swiped through the collection, her brow furrowed.

"Are you sure Bud is taking the money? Maybe he's giving it to this guy."

"I interviewed the bag man, and the guy who had him deliver the cash, so yeah, I'm sure. If you keep going, you'll see Morales is the one who ends up with the dough. And look where they are—a public restroom. They didn't want to be filmed."

"*La mordida,*" Doris said.

"What does that mean?"

"Literally it means a bite, but figuratively it's a bribe." She scoffed, and lowered her voice, so as not to be heard by the diners at the nearby tables. "So Bud is dirty."

"Extremely. That particular payoff was three hundred grand. Courtesy of a Chinese developer who wanted a variance on his luxury condo building. To keep the peasants out."

Still gazing at the screen, Doris's nose wrinkled. "Who are these two?"

Slater reached for the device. It was a photo of the straight couple in the restroom stall.

"The woman who was blackmailing Morales was also blackmailing one or both of them. I didn't actually talk to these people."

"What a sleazy way to make money."

"So what should I do with this?"

Doris sat back. "When I talked to Bud, I

thought it was about a woman. This isn't just a simple romantic faux pas."

"That's what he told me too. That someone had
photographic evidence of an affair. If these *mordida*
images got out, it would be much more damaging
than sex photos. He might get charged."

"It's not even like he's ripping off someone in a
shady business deal." Doris waved a hand. "He's an
elected official, so he's ripping off everyone."

Slater nodded. "That rings true."

She toyed with her fork, eyeing the boisterous
room for a moment before she spoke.

"You have to do the right thing," she said finally.
"You have to expose this."

"It might get traced back to me, and then to
you," Slater said. "Morales will know that I turned
him in."

"It doesn't matter. Some things are more important than friendships." She sighed. "Have you read
anything about the city's anticorruption rules?"

"No."

"There aren't any. At least none with teeth. The
local authorities won't be able to do anything with
this. It has to go to the feds."

Slater nodded. "I can arrange that."

"I need to talk to Bud. Will you come with me?"

"It'll save me a trip. I was going to have to talk
to him eventually."

"I'll tell him you got some results." Doris pulled
her phone out of her bag and thumb-typed, peering at the screen. "I bet he'll want to talk about it
tonight."

She waved down the waitress, and asked for the check. The woman produced it on the spot and handed it to her.

"Let me pay," Slater said. "I called the meeting."

"Thank you, sweetheart," she said, and handed it to him.

"Hold up," he called to the waitress, and pulled out his wad of cash, and handed her a sheaf of bills with the check.

Doris was gazing at her phone. "Bud wrote back. He wants to see you tonight."

"He's at city hall?"

"At his place. In Boyle Heights. We'll go together."

As she tucked her phone away, the guy at the next table leaned toward her. He was sitting beside Slater and facing Doris, wearing a stupid black driving cap.

In a thick British accent, he said, "Can you pass the sauce?"

Slater caught the meaning, but Doris didn't, as he pronounced *sauce* like "sews."

"Excuse me?" she said.

"The sauce, love. Am I not speaking English?"

"Right." She frowned, and handed him the little bottle of hot sauce from their table. To Slater, she said, "I'm going to wash my hands. Then we can go."

Slater pulled on his jacket and looked the guy over, then glanced at the woman he was with. She had shaggy red hair and a thick cable-knit sweater. It looked way too warm for this place, more appropriate for trekking in the Andes or going out on a shrimp boat. Gazing at her dinner companion, she had a smug smile on her face.

When Doris stepped out of view, Slater reached over and grabbed the guy's forearm, at the wrist and at the elbow, holding it inconspicuously below the level of the table.

"What the hell?" the guy demanded. His fork dropped onto his plate with a clatter.

"You don't get to condescend to her," Slater said, leaning closer.

"Let go of me."

Slater tightened his grip. "There are two little bones right here in your arm," he said quietly. "Feel that? You're going to step outside with me, nice and calm, or I'll break one and dislocate the other."

Slater rose, and the guy got up with him.

"Excuse us for a moment," he said to the woman.

Pushing the guy away from the table, Slater shifted his grip to his upper arm, so that what he was doing wouldn't be obvious to anyone who glanced at them. It was just a few steps to the exit door, and Slater hauled the guy outside.

"Dude—let go of me. What's your damage?"

Slater shoved him farther into the parking lot and spun him around. "What happened to the limey accent?"

"I'm practicing for an audition."

"That doesn't mean you get to be an asshole."

The guy tried to shrug his way out of Slater's grip. "From here it looks like you're the only asshole present."

Pulling back, Slater punched him in the face. The guy cried out and put a hand to his nose.

"Why do you make me do this to you?" Slater shouted, and gut-punched him.

He groaned and crumpled to the pavement, pulling his knees up to his chest. Slater took a step back, glaring at him, breathing hard. It took all his strength to resist kicking him in the kidneys. He forced himself to turn around and walk back inside.

The woman in the heavy sweater frowned at him as he approached the table.

"Where's Mike? He was only rehearsing for a part. Why did you freak out?"

"Does he not know how he sounds?" Slater demanded. "Words have consequences. That moron going all Cockney is like handing an eight-year-old a machine gun. Sure, that'll work out just fine."

"Where is he?"

"Mike said he doesn't love you anymore. I don't think he'll be back."

"I'm not his girlfriend, you dipshit. I'm his agent."

"He's a loser, sister, and you know it. Cut him loose."

Doris walked up, grinning at him, and said, "Where's the cheeky limey?"

"We should go," Slater said, and put a hand on the small of her back, and led her across the restaurant, out the side door to the parking lot.

"What's the hurry?" Doris said.

"Don't ask. Where's your car?"

"I took a ride-share. I wanted to have a margarita. They make such lovely ones here. They use fresh limes."

"So I'll drive."

Eyeing her as she climbed into the Thunderbird, she actually did seem a little tipsy. Doris was such a lightweight. One cocktail and she was over the legal limit.

"Does Morales know we're both coming?" he said, flicking on his headlights and pulling out onto Sunset.

"He will when we get there."

———·———

WHEN THEY PULLED UP at Morales's house, the only thing in view was a high fence. It looked expensive—horizontal redwood boards in a metal frame. He parked at the curb, and they climbed out. Doris led the way to the gate and rang the bell.

"This must be the biggest house in the neighborhood," Slater said.

"Bud bought two lots on this street, and the two behind them on the next street, and combined them all."

"It's like those obnoxious fortified compounds in Latin America."

"Obnoxious but necessary in those places," she said.

"Boyle Heights isn't one of those places. This guy is a damn gonif."

The lock on the gate buzzed, and Slater pushed it open. Lit by a series of short lampposts, a path led toward the house, through a rocky garden with clusters of stupid Mexican feathergrass. There were raised beds on both sides, lush with foliage, and Slater stooped to take a look. Primroses.

"Admiring the horticulture?" Doris said.

"His landscaper needs a psych eval."

"You don't approve?"

"This is a wrong plant. Although it's not the plant's fault—that's on some stupid human for putting it here."

At the house, a blocky modern structure, Morales stepped outside, booming out a cheery greeting. Such a politician. Tonight he was wearing a cream-colored sweater and dark trousers, like what a stylist would have chosen for casual Friday at an aspirational law firm.

"Hi, Bud," Doris called to him.

"Are you the primrose nut?" Slater said as they approached.

"What, now?"

He waved to the raised beds. "You've got, like, six genera of them here."

"I didn't choose the greenery, if that's what you're asking. I hire guys like you to do the garden."

"Guys like me." Slater scoffed. "You mean fungible blue-collar grunts."

"He means specialists," Doris said. "Calm down."

Slater waved his arm. "This is hilarious. You've planted a literal primrose path to your front door."

"OK," Morales said evenly. "Are you going to come inside?"

He led them into a foyer with a high ceiling and a dimly lit chandelier of cascading chunky glass, and then into a dark-paneled room with an obnoxiously huge leather sofa and oversize chairs. The fireplace had glowing embers in it, like a bland corporate hotel lobby. The table at the far end, near the windows, was actually a desk, Slater realized.

"Drink?" Morales said.

"No." Doris sat at one end of the sofa.

Slater waited for Morales to sit, then took the other chair.

"You lied to me, Bud," Doris said, leaning toward him. "The blackmail photos were nothing to do with a woman. You're on the take."

"Oh, dear." Morales sighed, then gestured widely. "It wasn't really a lie. I just softened it a little. You never moved beyond the classroom, Doris. You don't understand the big picture."

"After you bailed on public education, I worked as an administrator for many years. I wasn't living under a rock."

"This is about the wheels of commerce. You don't know how city business works. In LA, it's pay to play."

"Those photos aren't about doing business," she said. "They're about corruption."

"That's such an ugly word." Morales sat back and looked at Slater. "So you had to run to Mama to tattle. You had to tell her all about what you found. I thought you were working for me."

"Technically, she's the one who hired me."

"I'm the one who paid you."

"With a Chinese developer's bribe money, it seems," Slater said.

Morales's eyes went hard. After a moment he rose and stepped over to his desk.

"I think we can work this out," he said, and pulled open a drawer, then set two bricks of cash on the desktop.

They were new bills, Slater saw, still with the dark-yellow currency straps.

Morales eyed Doris. "That's twenty grand. I bet that'll sweeten your teacher's pension a little."

"Those are nice," Doris said, not budging from the sofa. "Where do you get them made?"

"It's real money, Doris. Take it."

"You can't buy me," she said, raising her voice.

Slater got up, and stepped over to the desk, and scooped up the bundles, stuffing them into his jacket pockets.

"What are you doing?" Doris demanded.

"Confiscating it," he said, meeting her gaze. "It's evidence now. Maybe we can trace it to its source."

"You're both being ridiculous." Morales put his hands on his hips and eyed Slater. "You just had to go and show Mama those photos. Did you manage to get hold of the originals?"

"I deleted them from Dawn's cloud drive. I assume that wiped them out completely. She might have copies stashed somewhere else, but I don't think she'll be bothering you again. She's in jail on a felony charge and not eligible for release."

"How did that happen?"

"I managed to get her popped for something

else," Slater said, gesturing vaguely.

"Like what?"

"The camera that caught you taking the bribe was set up to create urinal voyeur porn. She was selling it. I think that makes it a sex crime. She might do hard time."

"I wondered how she got those photos," Morales said. "There was no one there except for me and the button man, and restrooms aren't supposed to have cameras."

"I told you before that Dawn was already on parole for something else. She won't be back in the extortion business anytime soon."

"He's efficient, your son," Morales said.

"What did I tell you?"

He held Doris's gaze. "Are you going to make trouble for me?"

"You've done that to yourself." She stood up. "You can't take bribes, Bud. You know better."

"No one is going to believe you," he said, his tone sharp.

"I guess we'll see."

"We're leaving," Slater said. "Don't try to stop us, and don't come after either of us. If I don't get back to my computer tonight, those photos go out in an email blast to everyone I've ever met."

"You think I'd do that?" Morales demanded. "Doris is my lifelong friend. You think I'm a thug?"

"He's not a violent person, sweetie," Doris said, tapping his arm.

"I'm not so sure. If you back it into a corner, even a tame rat will go for the jugular."

Slater followed her into the foyer and out into the yard.

"Down the primrose path," he said, glancing back at the house as they walked toward the street.

"When do they bloom?"

"In the fall. Not for very long."

Once they'd climbed into the Thunderbird, Doris took a deep breath.

"It's all true. He didn't deny any of it."

"You thought he might?" Slater twisted the key in the ignition.

"I guess part of me hoped it was all some huge misunderstanding. That Bud would explain it all, and it would make sense, and we'd have a good laugh. But he copped to it."

"He totally copped to it." Slater flicked on his headlights and pulled into the street. "Unlike everything else, the truth is always self-consistent. No contradictions, no ill-fitting pieces. It stitches the world together. It's not always easy to hear, but from my experience, in the long run it's the most satisfying option."

"Listen to you—my son, the philosopher." She sighed. "I should have known something was up the last time I saw Bud and his wife. He was driving a snow-white Bentley, and her hands looked like they were on fire."

"You mean her jewelry?"

"There were more diamonds on her than in Antwerp." She waved a hand. "All this tsuris, and he dragged me into it."

"To be fair," Slater said, "he didn't want you

personally to do anything illegal. Not telling you the whole truth insulated you from that reality."

"Just give me a minute to think."

They rode in silence as Slater navigated the dark streets toward the freeway, then headed to Mount Washington. Pulling into her driveway, he was glad there was no sign of stupid Albert's stupid car.

"Come in for a minute," Doris said, and climbed out.

In the kitchen, Slater sat on a stool at the counter and watched as she absently opened two bottles of ginger beer, and handed him one. She took a sip and then braced her arms on the countertop, facing him.

"Do you know anyone in the FBI?" she said.

"Conrad does."

"You can't let Conrad be the intermediary. Bud was a cop. If he still has influence in the department, he can make it all disappear."

"That's a good insight." Slater eyed her appreciatively. "I'll get an intro and take it to them myself."

"Keep copies of everything in case someone there buries it."

"I talked to a journalist who wants the dirt on the middleman. The guy who was representing the developers. If I share it with her, it'll be a lot harder for it to get ignored."

"Good idea. Give the feds a week or so lead time before you talk to the journalist. Maybe warn them that it's going to break publicly. They'll tell you not to talk to the media, because it'll interfere with their investigation, but they can't stop you from doing that. If they know the scandal is coming, it will give them extra motivation to get out ahead of it."

"I have to say," Slater said, "I respect the way you're handling this."

She raised her eyebrows. "What's the number-one rule?"

It was something she'd first told him long ago, before he was even in grade school.

Slater tipped his bottle toward her. "We do the right thing."

———•———

A FEW WEEKS LATER, on a cold morning, Slater woke in bed, alone, and with a clear head. When he checked his phone, there was a text from Doris:

Word is out.

Her subsequent text was a link to a news item, titled "More City Hall Corruption Exposed." The byline read Nell Pilapil. She worked fast—Slater had just given her the photos and all the details a week or so ago.

After he'd talked to the feds, and given them the images, and explained what he knew of the story, Doris had nudged him about the twenty grand he'd taken from Morales, and reminded him that he had to turn it in. But in Slater's mind, taxing a couple of racks from a thief wasn't really problematic. Besides, the money was from a sleazy developer, and the project approval it had purchased would be derailed now, whether he turned in the cash or not. Slater had done the legwork, dealt with the trash, uncovered the sleaze. The feds had just breezed in at the end to take all the credit and file charges. He had more right to the cash than some bottomless federal evidence fund.

Reading through the article, he scrolled past the familiar photo of Morales taking the bales of cash from Baglio, then Morales's official portrait, beaming like an idiot with the city flag in the background, and stopped at a photo captioned "Morales's vehicle vandalized this morning."

The image depicted a white Bentley, parked at a curb somewhere, spray-painted along the driver's side in fluorescent orange with the word VENDIDO in big blocky letters. The paint had run in places— it clearly wasn't the work of a practiced graffiti artist. There was a can of spray paint in that color in Doris's toolshed. He'd used it to outline projects on the ground in her yard, to give her a visual sense of his landscaping plans.

Thinking about it, though, this didn't seem like Doris, such a brazen act of vandalism. But he'd heard her use that word, one of many she'd picked up over the years working with Spanish-speaking kids and educators. He'd heard it before, and he knew what it meant: "sellout."

———•———

Also from Dagmar Miura

That First Heady Burn

The first book in the Slater Ibáñez series sees Slater running surveillance on an injured tech worker and tangling with blackmailers, party girls, late-night hookups with a gamut of guys, and a lot of bourbon.

slater.dagmarmiura.com

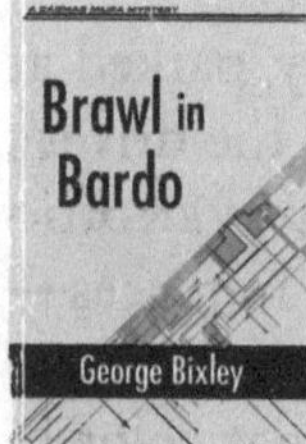

Brawl in Bardo

Slater spends the night in a dusty Mojave Desert town and finds that things look different in the liminal space between LA and Vegas, like the *bardo* between lives. Soon he's stalking a sleazy dermatologist who's in a custody battle with another croaker for a seemingly worthless statue.

slater.dagmarmiura.com

The Mason Braithwaite Paranormal Mystery Series

No one is ever quite sure whether psychic investigator Mason gets results with actual psychic power or his more mundane flatfooting, but the disheveled redhead manages to resolve some intractable mysteries.

mason.dagmarmiura.com

Penstock Canyon

While helping out a friend suffering from late-night visitations, psychic investigator Mason is confronted with aliens on the roof and mythical beings that have him questioning the very nature of reality.

mason.dagmarmiura.com

Truman and Celeste

Sometimes all a woman needs is a decent man—even if she's not sleeping with him. Join Truman and Celeste as they troll the gritty underbelly of Los Angeles, never hesitating to slam that cocktail, hit on guys, or ask the next relevant question.

truman.dagmarmiura.com

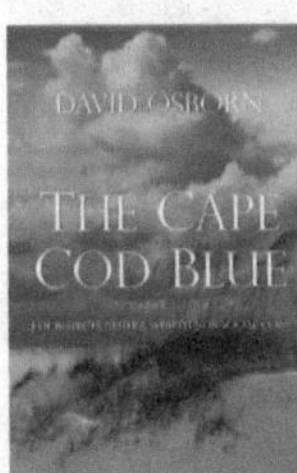

The Cape Cod Blue

The glittering, exalted world of art auctioning hides love, hate, and parricidal murder in a wealthy and socially prominent family when forgery of an anonymous Cape Cod painting is used to steal a world-famous portrait that's worth a fortune.

capecod.dagmarmiura.com

The Bone Bridge

Yarrott Benz, the 2016 Ippy Award winner for memoir, is forced to deal with extraordinary self-sacrifice in this harrowing account of teenage brothers, as different as night and day, trapped together in a dramatic medical dilemma.

bonebridge.dagmarmiura.com

The Psychic Vegan Cookbook

It has never been easier to cook vegan, and you don't even need to be psychic to do it. Whether your motivation is eating healthier or the welfare of other sentient creatures, Henrietta Flores guides you through plant-based versions of familiar dishes.

cookbook.dagmarmiura.com